KINDRED
Spirits

Short fiction and poetry by the
Infinite Monkeys Chapter of the League of Utah Writers

Kindred Spirits
— Short Fiction and Poetry by the Infinite Monkeys
Chapter of the League of Utah Writers

Anthology Copyright © 2023
  by The Infinite Monkeys Genre Writers Corporation

Individual works are Copyright © 2023 by their respective authors

ISBN-13: 978-1-7325836-4-1 (Paperback)
ISBN-13: 978-1-7325836-5-8 (Ebook)

Library of Congress Control Number: 2023905256

Edited by:
  Danielle Harward, Talysa Sainz, Johnny Worthen & Dan Yocom

Managing Editor:
  Talysa Sainz

Layout by:
  Johnny Worthen

Cover design © 2023 The Infintie Monkeys Genre Writers
Cover design by RebeccaCovers.

This book is a work of fiction. Names, characters, places, and incidents either are products of the author's imagination or are used fictitiously. Any resemblance to actual events or locales or persons, living or dead, is entirely coincidental and not intended by the authors.

All rights reserved. Except as permitted under the U.S. Copyright Act of 1976, no part of this publication may be reproduced, distributed, or transmitted in any form or by any means, or stored in a database or retrieval system, without the prior permission of the publisher.

CONTENTS

INTRODUCTION
Daniel Yocom   1

SECRET SOCIETY OF THE MASTER'S SEVEN MUSES
Inna V. Lyon   3

PAESANI
Whitney Oliver   20

I'M NOT SARAH
Gina G   28

A WICKED KILT
Amanda Hill   42

A CHRISTMAS MEMORY
Pat Patridge   53

THOSE WHO HAUNT THE NIGHT
C.H. Lindsay   61

THE HAMMER CLUB
Johnny Worthen   62

THE COLLECTION
Talysa Sainz   71

AIDEEN
Edward Matthews   83

JUST DESSERTS
Katrina Hayes   98

MAN'S BEST FRIEND
Lori Shields   102

MORNING MEDITATION
Scott Bryan   107

TO NEW LIVES
Daniel Yocom — *111*

THE LAST GOODNIGHT
Steve Prentice — *119*

TODAY, TOMORROW AND THE NEXT
Jessica Zarnofsky — *120*

ADVENTURE AWAITS
Rashelle Yeates — *129*

FATE AND KARMA MEET FOR COFFEE
Candace Thomas — *144*

A FUTURE TOLD
Logan Sidwell — *153*

CHALLENGE ACCEPTED
Danielle Harward — *164*

AFTERWORD
Bryan Young — *178*

ABOUT THE AUTHORS — *181*

INTRODUCTION

Dan Yocom

We look for connections to people and the world around us. That association may be a surface level of having some of the same likes in music, art, reading, or other areas of interest. When a deeper link is found with another person, we call them a kindred spirit. That is what this is—a collection of stories about the deeper bond found, by a gathering of authors who have found relationships between each other.

The stories, poetry, and an essay in this book explore the theme of finding that deeper level of connection with others. There are ones about having a common interest, while others are about finding a soulful link to those who are similar in other ways. There is the link to our own past and to the past we have learned about, or the bond of being in a setting at the same time.

Not all connections are for the better. Some raise our hopes, others concern us. Not every doppelganger or like-minded thinker we connect with will raise us to a greater good. As angels are brought together, so are demons. Almost always, the relationship will provide us with a better understanding of ourselves, if not the world.

Be prepared to read these works and understand many are holding a mirror to the society we live in. The reflection may be greatly warped like the mirrors in the carnival fun house, or only slightly. There are also those that have tints to the glass that provide a darker view. In each, there is something more than what is initially seen.

Each piece is an original work from members of the League

of Utah Infinite Monkeys Genre Writers Chapter—a group of writers with talents ranging in style, form, and experience. There are more members of our troop than what is represented. We learn from each other and teach the skills we can to those who are eager to become better writers and authors.

We welcome those who may find they share the spirit of creating written works. You are our kindred spirits in the journey of sharing our tales, memories, dreams, and even nightmares. You can find out more about the Infinite Monkeys Genre Writers at the following locations:

Website: https://luwgenremonkeys.wordpress.com/

Facebook: https://www.facebook.com/groups/LUWInfiniteMonkeys

League of Utah Writers Website: https://www.leagueofutahwriters.com/

If you enjoy this work, please leave a review for others to read on your favorite book sites. Most of the authors included in this collection have additional work available in other Infinite Monkeys Anthologies or published through other means.

I thank you for supporting our group by reading this work.

Daniel Yocom
President, The LUW Infinite Monkeys Genre Writers

SECRET SOCIETY OF THE MASTER'S SEVEN MUSES

Inna V. Lyon

A black Citroën C-Crosser slowed down at the address of 5 Rue de Thorigny. Headlights caught a blue sign: "National Picasso Museum—Paris. Open from 10:30 a.m. to 6:00 p.m." Normally, a visit to the popular museum wouldn't arouse suspicion, but the time was approaching midnight.

The fresh April night smelled of the chestnut trees blossoming.

An ancient dark blue door in the stone wall opened, and a young man in a gray suit slipped onto the sidewalk. He opened the car door and helped an elderly lady step out of the vehicle.

"Madame Salk," muttered the young man, kissing her wrinkled hand.

"André, please, no names. Let this visit remain a secret," the lady replied in French.

"Yes, of course, I'm sorry."

She patted the young man on the shoulder. She was short and fragile and wore a stylish red cardigan, black pants, and black flats. Short black hair framed her wrinkled face, high forehead, and painted eyebrows. A pointed nose, a small, pursed mouth, and flabby cheeks that accompanied her once dazzling smile now hung like two used tea bags. Her eyes were sharp and penetrating despite their appearance.

André held open the door, and both proceeded over the cobblestone courtyard to the heavy doors of the main entrance.

The old lady leaned on the young man's folded arm.

They entered the hall of the museum, the former Hôtel Salé, when André whispered into the woman's ear, "How was the anniversary, Madame?"

"Ah, André, when you are a hundred years old, you feel like a forgotten painting in an abandoned workshop. Strangers, whose names you don't remember, would applaud, and give you useless presents and empty speeches. And those who you would want to see have long rested in peace."

They passed the first two halls and entered a long, spacious room. The moonlight captured the barely distinguishable paintings on the walls. In the middle of the room stood a row of four uncomfortable modern benches for visitors who wanted to take a break from miles of art. A deep, comfortable armchair that didn't belong to the modern interior of the exhibition hall stood facing Picasso's painting Women Running on the Beach. The old lady sank into the armchair's blue cushion.

"May I bring something for you, Madame? Tea? Water? Chardonnay?"

"No, André, thank you. Wait for me outside. I would like to be alone with the past and Pablo's paintings."

"Of course, Madame."

The young man bowed and quietly withdrew. The lady waited for the sound of the massive front door to close, echoing through the empty halls.

She'd lied about her reason for the night visit to the museum. Even though it was the anniversary of Picasso's death, Madame was not going to mourn the famous painter. She never called him Master or Genius. To her, he was always just Pablo. She'd also lied about being alone.

The old woman took out a fan from her black handbag and fanned herself a couple of times. The air was stuffy.

"Olga, I'm not going to play hide-and-seek with you. I still have things to do in this world. Where are the rest?"

A transparent white figure swam in the direction of the chair and stopped in front of the French woman. Hovering above the floor was a nocturnal ghost, a departed soul, an ephemeral creature woven from the air and silvery filaments of moonlight. The vague silhouette outlined large arrogant facial features, a full figure, and a ballerina tutu comically fastened to her like a saddle on a cow.

"Olga, I beg you—not today. Please, change into something more appropriate for the occasion."

The outline of the tutu changed to a tight-fitting dress with a large brooch at the shoulder, but the full figure and pursed lips remained the same. The ghost spoke in French, her Russian accent strong.

"I just wanted to show these three fools that the soul that has departed in a Christian way is capable of changing her appearance. A person who took her own life would be denied such privilege."

"Your sarcasm only applies to Maria-Thérèse and Jacqueline; that would be two . . ." She wanted to say "fools" but stopped herself. It wouldn't be wise to start an important meeting with a small quarrel, especially since she never knew which ghosts had already descended.

"But Dora?" gasped Olga.

"Madness is not suicide," replied the old woman, fanning herself. The air conditioners maintained the microclimate temperature of the museum for paintings but not for her old post-menopaused body.

"Still a sinner. You all are sinners and prostitutes. You jumped into my lawful husband's bed as soon as he waved his brush."

"Not jumped, but surrendered to the sacrificial podium of his art," a new voice whispered, followed by someone else's hysterical laughter.

Two more transparent figures floated into the room through the wall. They were Maria-Thérèse and Dora, once ardent rivals but now inseparable soulmates. The first was nude, voluptuous, with a scrap of rope around her neck. The second was tall and skinny, emphasized by the shapeless straitjacket that hung from her body.

Olga stuck her tongue out at the new arrivals. They hissed in reply.

"Ladies, behave yourselves. Our agenda has important issues that require your participation, experience, and opinion."

"Oh, do you still need the secrets we took with us to the grave?" asked Maria-Thérèse in a high, languid voice.

"Where are Jacqueline, Fernande, and Marcelle?" Madame asked, answering a question with a question.

A sad voice came from the corner, "I'm here. I've been here for a while, listening to your vulgarities." The figure of the last wife of the Master, Jacqueline Roque, swam out of her hiding place only for a moment before dissolving again into the darkness.

The old woman slammed her folded fan on the handle of the chair. "Enough is enough. We can bicker all night. You all know that Pablo was incapable of loving one woman. Each era of his art required new inspiration. And we gave him that inspiration, getting in return everything each of us wanted. So, calm down. We have bigger matters to discuss tonight."

Madame took a much-needed calming breath. Tonight would be rough, given the meeting's matters. She nodded to a figure in the corner opposite Jacqueline's hiding place. "Greetings, Fernande. Where is Marcelle?"

"Where else should she be? Sobbing in the next room near the painting Woman in Tears," snorted Olga.

"How poetic," Maria-Thérèse sang.

"And romantic," Dora echoed her.

They both burst into laughter, swirling in a whirlwind, creating a jet of cool air.

"I'll call the poor girl." Jacqueline disappeared into the wall without being asked.

Puffing with anger, Olga swam to another corner but found the cloud of unhappy Fernande there and retreated to sit on the bench near Madame.

The fuzzy shadows of Maria-Thérèse and Dora approached the painting of women running along the beach, and they spread themselves across, imitating the shapes on the canvas. Dora exposed her left breast as the woman in the front. Maria-Thérèse, already naked, had nothing to bare and only grabbed Dora's hand, lifting it above her head as Picasso's picture depicted.

Olga muttered something in Russian, but no one wanted a translation.

A minute later, Jacqueline and Marcelle appeared in the room. Jacqueline took her place in the corner, covering her chest with both hands. The fragile figure of Marcelle appeared before the elderly lady.

"Madame, I apologize for being late. My heart is washed with tears every time I see Master's painting. But my soul wants to rush back to heaven where I can sit at the gates of his house."

Olga hushed her. "Shhh. No details about heaven for the living."

The elderly lady smiled to herself and stretched out her hand to Marcelle in greeting.

"My child, thank you for your appearance today. I understand how hard it is for you to break away from the affairs of heaven." Then she looked around the room. She straightened her back, preparing mentally for this to go awry. "Well, if everyone is assembled, then I declare the meeting of the Secret Society of the Master's Seven Muses opened. I have two items of business for discussion. Let's start with the most important one." She paused for effect. "Guernica is in danger."

"What?"

"It can't be."

"How is that possible?"

All spoke at the same time. The air in the room shook from the ghosts' movement.

Jealousy, bragging, and competition disappeared, giving way to the real concern and unity of these restless souls. Despite the rivalry for the Master's love, his art remained that unifying component for this group of women calling themselves the Secret Society of the Master's Seven Muses. Their past lives and destinies, tragic and unhappy, had been intertwined with artistic periods in Pablo's career as an artist. Fernande may have inspired Picasso at the beginning of cubism, but Dora championed Guernica, and she was proud of it. The mural-sized masterpiece, the apotheosis of his tens of thousands of pieces, was finished in only thirty-five days. Pablo was outraged and inspired by the bombing of the town of Guernica in the province of Basque. It remained the pinnacle of Pablo's artistry, even to the muses themselves.

Displayed in the Spanish pavilion at the fair of 1937, the painting saw the backs of visitors and received a controversial response. Only after many years of touring Europe and the United States did the mural gain public recognition and become a symbol of anti-war protest for the people of the world.

Olga's voice shouted over all the other women's voices.

"Is someone going to steal it? After all, the Master's canvases remain the most popular among art thieves."

Madame folded her hands. "Olga, don't be silly. Who would try to steal an eleven-by-twenty-five-foot canvas protected by bulletproof glass and an advanced alarm?"

"Then what?" asked Marcelle in a broken voice.

"They're moving it. Yes, moving. Transportation from one museum to another. It's going to destroy the canvas," the matron's steady voice was followed by Marcelle's relieved sobs. "The painting was created for the commission of the Spanish Republic and rightfully belongs to them. But in his will, Pablo indicated that the painting should be exhibited at the Prado Museum in Madrid."

"But the canvas was in the Prado if I remember correctly," Olga said.

"You don't. Guernica was moved from the Prado Museum to the Reina Sofia Art Center thirty years ago," growled Dora. She considered herself the most important muse and inspiration during the creation of the piece. She lived with Pablo during the war with Spain and, being a photographer, took a detailed photo history of the masterpiece's creation. Although, she was not the only muse in those years. There were rumors of

Dora and Maria-Thérèse fighting over Pablo's love in his studio. No doubt, Dora won since the other woman wouldn't give any details of that squabble.

"That's true. Guernica is at the Reina Sofia Art Center in Madrid," the elderly lady continued. "But now a new Guggenheim Museum has been built in Bilbao, and Basque nationalists are negotiating the return of the painting to its official homeland. They organized the 'Guernica to Basque' movement, claiming to have letters written by Picasso during the Spanish War of 1937. Picasso financially supported the National Front and promised the Spanish Communists that Guernica would return to its historical homeland."

The women listened with bated breath. Apparently, earthly news didn't reach the heavens as quickly as it dispersed in this world.

Madame continued. "After years of touring Europe and more than forty years in the United States, the canvas has worn out due to frequent transportation and repeated stretching. There is a significant risk of damage. First, Guernica won't be able to handle another move. Second, no matter how beautiful and modern the museum in Bilbao is, Madrid should remain its home as Pablo wanted."

All the battles between the women were in the past. Madame, after separating from the artist, had developed a strong vocabulary for her former lover where the "old stubborn ass" was the mildest of all. She had spent years in legal fights with Jacqueline for that crazy fool's inheritance and surname for her children, citing the artist's mental state since he did not want to provide for his own children and grandchildren. But jealousy and resentment between the women lost their relevance, the court division of money and properties ended, and past emotions subsided. Today was about something bigger and more significant for future generations. It required joint efforts.

Madame went on.

"Mateo Alvares, the grandson of a Basque nationalist, found a letter in his grandfather's archive and started the movement about relocating the painting to Bilbao's Museum. The letter hasn't been accessible to the public yet. A special committee was established."

"Who is on the committee?" asked Maria-Thérèse.

She and Dora left the canvas of women running along the beach and sat with the others on benches in the middle of the hall. Marcelle too. All except Jacqueline and Fernande, who never left their dark corners.

"There are five votes. A Frenchman, the same one who participated in the negotiations to return the canvas from the U.S. Museum of Modern Art back to Spain. Then, Mateo Alvares, who found the letters. They will vote for moving Guernica to Bilbao."

A nervous chill and whisper ran through their shaky figures.

"An American art historian from the U.S. Holocaust Memorial Museum. Also, my children and I are on the committee, but we have one vote for three of us."

"But it's not fair," Dora said. "You have every right to three votes. You are his family, direct descendants and living heirs."

"This is done to diminish our role," Madame replied in an even voice, detached from the whirlwind of anger toward the committee raging inside her. Disappointment or not, at least she had a vote.

"Who is the fifth?" asked Fernande, quieting the whirlwind in Madame for a moment. Since the rule for suicide sinners did not apply to Fernande, her transparent ghost trembled in the air in the form of a young French woman in a long dress as Pablo saw her in 1901.

It was clear to everyone that the fifth vote would be crucial.

"He or she? Basque or Madrid citizen?" Fernande sat down on the bench.

"Neither. It's a robot," Madame replied.

Bedlam ensued.

"Nonsense."

"It can't be. You are wrong."

"How can you entrust such an important decision to a robot?"

"Modern technology can. The robot is a four-meter camera that moves along the painting, takes pictures, and analyzes the conditions of the paints and the canvas itself." Madame heaved a sigh. She didn't like this robot any more than the other women, but she continued. "The robot was launched in January, and it will work until the end of May. Because of the sensitivity of the device and the purity of the analysis, the robot takes pictures at night and during the weekend when the museum is empty and there are no stomping visitors. Unfortunately, according to my sources, it has already shot several hundred thousand pictures and predicts that the piece is not in such a deplorable state as everyone feared," Madame concluded, melancholy tugging at her heart. If only she and her children had three votes.

She regretted now not asking André for a glass of wine. Stuffy air and long speeches parched her throat, and a headache bloomed behind her eyes.

Everyone was silent.

Madame looked around at the transparent ghostly figures—the former muses of the ruthless Master. They'd all had their fair share of suffering and misfortune. Fernande languished in a miserable existence after parting with Picasso until the day she died. Tiny Marcelle died at the age of twenty of tuberculosis in a hospital. Olga, the first official wife, died in poverty after Picasso left her. Maria-Thérèse had committed suicide in the garage of her home. Dora had ended up at the insane asylum. And Jacqueline, who took her life on the eve of the opening of the very museum where they were meeting tonight. Life lost all color for all of them after parting with the Master, and only Madame could boast that she had left Pablo by her choice. She made life on her own—built a career as an artist, raised children, married twice, and was still in the land of the living.

But what was there to brag about? Her days were numbered, celebrating her one-hundredth birthday. She had no illusions for another jubilee and was waiting for her turn to join the others.

She was here today, and no matter how much the other women wanted to help, she would have to do the job. Guernica was a masterpiece worth saving. These days, as never before, the painting represented a symbol of the struggle against oppression and disenfranchisement, a reminder of the horrors of war and lawlessness. Multiple copies around the world gave the original Guernica the right to be saved for future generations as an artistic treasure of freedom. The painting's fate was up to Madame and her alone.

"But we can help the robot to analyze the precious canvas," Marcelle whispered. Everyone looked back at the tiny figure of a young woman, for the first time seeing a mischievous smile instead of a sad and teary face. "After all, there is no one in the museum at night except for ghosts."

"Of course," Maria-Thérèse quipped. "We will be glad to help the sensitive robot assess the fragility of the picture."

Dora laughed. "For purity of the analysis."

"What can you do besides scaring the night watchman?" asked Madame.

Dora winked at Maria-Thérèse. They grabbed each other's hands and raced around the perimeter of the room again and again. A laughing Marcelle joined them, then plump Olga, and, lastly, Fernande herself. Five female figures, ghosts, spirits, former mistresses, and rivals rushed around the room, creating air currents. First, a slight breeze, then a decent draft, and finally, a whirlwind swept across the room, making the wall paintings tremble.

Ghostly disruption of the sensitive robot certainly could work. Madame breathed a sigh of relief, enjoying the refreshed air and sudden solution to the problem.

"What about you, Jacqueline? Don't you want to join the girls?" Madame turned to the corner where the transparent ghost was hiding. As Picasso's last legal wife, she'd shared with the Master not only abundant life and love pleasures but also his last years of disabilities and eccentricities.

"I have stronger arguments."

"Unexpected," said Madame. She raised her hand, urging the other ladies to calm down. "What do you propose?"

Jacqueline was silent. Her face moved forward to the light, but the figure remained in shadow. Because she took her life, she couldn't change her ghostly appearance and had to carry the cross of her last decision to take her life. In her face was torment, suffering, peace, appeasement, and detachment from worldly affairs all at the same time. Fifty-nine suited her. No wonder Picasso dedicated over 400 paintings to her.

"There are documents and records," Jacqueline said without raising her voice.

The women whispered, looked at each other, and sat down again on the benches for visitors. Dora stayed standing and swam in the direction of Jacqueline, who didn't flee back into the corner.

"All the secrets and diaries were made public long ago," Dora said. "His whole life, from the first naïve drawings of pigeon legs to personal correspondence, has long belonged to the public." She considered herself an expert in this field and had read all available memoirs about the Master.

"Things keep popping up. The letter of Basque patriot just showed up, right?"

Jacqueline looked at Madame, who nodded.

"What's in the documents?" pressed Dora.

"In the last years of his life, Pablo . . ." Jacqueline trailed off, then gathered herself and continued, "had regrets and remorse, if you can call it that. Several letters and entries in his last diaries are devoted to his repentance."

"But he was blind towards the end of his life and could neither paint nor write," Dora said, disbelief in her voice that Jacqueline hid something from her and the others. That was what the Society was for—to have all their secrets out to keep Pablo's legacy going.

"That's right. I wrote them under his dictation," Jacqueline continued.

"But what does this have to do with Guernica?" asked Madame. Dread was building in her stomach. What new skeletons from the closet of Pablo's vicious life could come forth and harm the living? She was terrified.

"While the masterpiece of his life was in the United States, its copies began to appear in Berlin, Dresden, and Hiroshima. Unprecedented pride had filled his heart as he realized the importance of Guernica as a humanitarian symbol of the struggle against modern warfare. Under his dictation, I wrote his resignation of the promise to the Communist Party to place Guernica in the Basque Country."

"But why haven't you ever said that before?" demanded Dora.

"Why would I? After all, eight years after the death of Pablo, Guernica returned to Spain. Bilbao or Madrid—I didn't care—I'm a Frenchwoman."

"But these are just diary entries. Not an official signed document," said Fernande.

"A notary showed up during Pablo's last summer. I managed to get a few of Pablo's last affairs notarized—the refusal letter included," replied Jacqueline.

Despite Jacqueline's dispassionate face and flat voice, general joy overcame every woman. They spoke all at once, flew from one to another, some even embraced.

But Madame knew it couldn't be that easy. "Wait."

The other ladies quieted.

"Where are these documents?" Madame asked in a hoarse voice, her parched throat needing drink and rest.

"Not far from here. In the deposit box at the Barclays Paris Bank on Rue de Turenne."

"And the key to the box?"

"At the Picasso Museum in Antibes," Jacqueline replied.

"In Antibes?" Now it was the time for Madame to worry. After all, it was a segment of her life with Pablo. There, on the second floor of the museum in the Château Grimaldi, she'd spent several months of her turbulent life with Pablo, where they lived, loved, painted, and where he was reborn as a master and artist. The couple left the castle after a few months, but Pablo had donated a collection of paintings, ceramics, drawings, and private items to the museum.

"So, the safety deposit box is in Paris, and the key to it is in Antibes?" asked Olga.

"Exactly," Jacqueline replied. "The box was opened in my name and paid for the next hundred years until 2085. The key to the box is in the Antibes Museum. I think you are familiar with the curator."

Everyone knew Jacqueline had committed suicide the night before the opening of Picasso's big exhibition in Paris. She outlived him by thirteen years, mostly alone, but before she could put a bullet in her chest, she'd settled all his affairs as the keeper of his vast inheritance and legacy. Or nearly all of them, it seemed.

"But why is it there?" asked Olga.

"My daughter from my first marriage inherited the villa of Notre-Dame-de-Vie where I lived, but she sold it to some millionaire. All my personal belongings were transferred to Antibes, along with the key. I hoped to bury all the mysteries forever. But . . ." Jacqueline stumbled.

"Tonight is the time to open the wardrobes filled with old skeletons," Dora finished for her.

"If this saves Guernica from moving south, then I will set free all the skeletons," Jacqueline said firmly.

For a moment, there was silence in the room. Each woman thought about her time with the Master, her own marks in history and art, regrets, and fate. Whether they were the ephemeral ghost or living flesh and blood, the Master's tenacious fingers wouldn't let them go too far from his multifaceted life and work. Such were the fates of geniuses and their followers.

"What about the second item of business?" reminded Olga.

"Oh yeah." The rest of the women perked up and looked to Madame.

Madame was so tired that she was ready to forget the second issue, but the others weren't. She leaned back in her chair and announced, "One person, through the press and the support of social media, is trying to add her name to Pablo's fame and publish a memoir called My Meetings with Pablo."

The women exchanged worried glances.

"Who is this person?" asked Maria-Thérèse.

"You know her. 1954," Madame replied wearily.

"Oh, no. Not the blonde ponytail," Dora groaned.

"Exactly, the ponytail."

A series of forty portraits of a slender girl with a high ponytail appeared in Picasso's works in 1954 and instantly became a topic of controversial debate—was she the subject of his passion or a purely platonic muse? The woman herself did not reveal the secret.

"Forty portraits are not that many. Paintings dedicated to us numbered in hundreds. Jacqueline alone is worth a fortune." Marcelle nodded in Jacqueline's direction.

"And the price tags too. Algerian Women sold for $175 million," Fernande added. "He never parted with the theme of cubism." She was terribly proud to be one of the few muses who captured three creative periods of Picasso and the beginning of cubism.

"The painting Dream with my image was sold for $155 million. Also, a decent value." Maria-Thérèse laughed.

"My portrait with a cat went off the auction for $96 million to the Russian billionaire," Dora retorted.

"Georgia is not Russia," Olga corrected, "it was bought by a Georgian billionaire."

"What's the difference?" said Dora as she wove the transparent kitten from the painting out of thin air.

Madame sighed. The women were incorrigible. Five minutes ago, they united in solving one big problem about Guernica, but now they were back to bragging and bickering.

"What do we do about the ponytail?" reminded Jacqueline.

"Is she intended to become a member of our Secret Society of the Master's Muses?" asked Dora. The kitten disappeared with the wave of her hand.

"Who knows. I think it will be up to posterity to decide," Madame replied. "Maybe in her book, she will answer the question that worries art historians and everyone else: who was she for Pablo?"

Madame glanced at her wrist. The large square display of the electronic clock showed 12:58 p.m.

"This meeting is adjourned," she said. "The Society's next meeting will be in October for his birthday anniversary in Malaga."

"In the meantime, we're going to visit Guernica, right, girls?" laughed Olga.

"Good luck with the robot," said Madame, "or rather—blow him away."

Madame smiled, musing aloud, "Perhaps I will have departed from this mortal body by then and will be able to join the Society of Seven Muses in a different state."

"You've been saying that for decades, old dog." Dora laughed and disheveled Madame's veiny hairstyle by flying over her head.

Seconds later, the floor clock in the next room chimed 1:00 a.m. The ghostly figures of the women melted into the semi-darkness, leaving behind a light plume of cool air.

The elderly Madame lifted her stiff, fragile body from the deep chair. Damn old age—everything hurts. She was about to leave the hall when the last figure emerged from the corner. Jacqueline stood before the old lady. Her chest was torn apart by a bullet, and if the blood did not ooze from the wound anymore, it was only because life had long since left the torn flesh yet. Still, her aspect captured the last agony of her tragic moment.

"Wait," the broken woman whispered.

Madame stopped. "Anything else?"

"The deposit box holds one more secret. Along with documents and diaries, you will find a bunch of letters. He dictated them in the last year of his life. They are addressed to all his women. These were never made public or sent to the recipients," she said.

"What's in those letters?" Madame lifted a brow.

"Repentance. Tears. Depression. Longing for the departed. Proof that he wasn't an insensitive monster as many painted him."

"Letters for all seven?"

"For eight. You will find the answer to our second discussion there."

Madame's eyebrows crept up. "Do you mean the blonde ponytail?"

"Yes. I wanted to destroy all these letters immediately after his death. But I didn't."

The women were silent.

Jacqueline, still covering the wound on her chest, approached Madame.

"You must decide what to do with them. Goodbye for now."

The white figure of the martyr approached the window, where moonlight touched her silhouette.

"Jacqueline. One question." Madame paused, hesitating. "How's it going up there?" she pointed upwards. "Do you see him?"

A gentle smile lit up the face of the once-strong woman.

"Franny. You know that you're asking the impossible. We keep a non-disclosure vow about life in heaven. Besides, you will soon find out for yourself."

Madame grinned and nodded. It was true. No one lives forever, except maybe those with fame. Picasso will live forever through his art, and they would, too.

"Blonde ponytail. What should I do about her?"

Jacqueline smiled again.

"I think seven is a good number. The Seven Wonders of the World, the Seven Sins, the Seven Primary Colors of the Palette."

Madame nodded. A journey to Antibes, a phone call to her lawyer, and the meeting of the committee to decide the fate of Guernica lay ahead. The last page of Pablo's history must be turned. Perhaps, not the last.

What did that one art magazine once say about Pablo? Picasso wrote our fates in advance. Everything we love will be lost.

Madame packed her fan and left the hall. There was much to do—spiritual retirement had to wait. Tomorrow was not guaranteed to anyone . . . unless you had the Secret Society's membership paid forward.

PAESANI

Whitney Oliver

Paesani. *A person who shares one's place of origin; a compatriot, especially among Italians or people of Italian descent.*

In my eighth grade Family and Consumer Science (FACS) class, we were given the all-too-popular assignment of bringing in food that represents our heritage. Easy. My Grandpa Marrelli is Italian. Done.

He rarely cooked, so I spent the evening before the assignment was due with my Grandma Marrelli. Martha Gayle (Bendall) Marrelli, my grandma, and the daughter of Welsh immigrants.

I asked her to teach me a family recipe to take to class. She taught me how to make her famous deviled eggs. She's known for them in my family. She brings them to every family gathering. The "secret" ingredients were passed down to her from her mother. To her mother from her grandmother.

It wasn't until years later that I understood why my FACS teacher watched me present the food from my Italian heritage with a tilted head and a confused expression. My Grandma Marrelli was obviously–though not to me at the time–not Italian. She only married one.

It didn't even occur to me I brought something that didn't make sense. I'm honestly not sure when I learned that my Grandma Marrelli didn't share any of the Italian blood I so readily claimed.

My inner critic often questions why, from the time I was in elementary school and still to this day, I identify as a member of a heritage group that I claim through only 25% of my DNA. Growing up, I celebrated no Italian traditions, spoke no Italian, and ate absolutely zero authentic Italian food.

Melanei Holtz said it best in the intro to her Italian Genealogy Guide: "Something in my DNA knew I was Italian before I did."

Two years after high school graduation, my prefrontal cortex had (thankfully) developed enough to open up space for more important things than the color of my backpack, my most recent crush, and whether or not people could see the grade on my paper when my teacher returned it. I developed a little more cultural awareness and curiosity. My desire to know about what it meant to be Italian grew. Though the act of actually doing the finding stayed low on my priority list.

Then Grandpa Marrelli was diagnosed with Myasthenia Gravis and spent a month in the ICU on a ventilator. We didn't think he was going to make it. The guilt of having spent years wanting to know more about him, without carving out the time to ask, hit me hard.

When it was clear we'd get a little more time with him, I had a burning desire to learn as much as I could before I lost the chance forever. I spent Thanksgiving of 2014 in the hospital with him, recording his voice as I pestered him with questions about his life, his childhood, his parents.

I learned about the schools he attended, the sports he played, and the jobs he worked. I learned about the offer he got to play professional football and his career at the Rio Grande Railroad. An improvement from the life of a miner his father experienced.

Later that year, I worked as a secretary in the Chemistry Department at the University of Utah. One of the professors I worked for hired a post-doc from Italy. I told her of my Italian grandfather, trying to connect with her, casually joking I was the only blonde-haired, blue-eyed Italian I knew. She gave me the same look my FACS teacher gave me but was too polite to say anything.

At that point, I didn't realize that just because my sister, my mom, my grandpa, and the rest of the Italians in Helper, Utah are olive-skinned, with dark hair and dark eyes that not all people in Italy were.

I still feel shame in the pit of my stomach when I think how uninformed I must have sounded. How my attempts to connect with her probably made me seem like a fraud who claimed roots in a country I clearly knew nothing about. How I didn't even realize that my attempts at connecting with my heritage were still juvenile.

My grandpa passed away a short year later. I have since learned the questions I wish I would have asked him before he passed away. What was it like being the son of Italian immigrants in America? Did your mom or dad talk about Italy? Were there any Italian traditions practiced in your home growing up? Your dad came to America by himself at age fifteen—did he ever tell you about his experience? Why did he end up in Southeastern Utah, of all places? Did your parents ever speak English? Do you know how to speak Italian? Were you proud to be Italian growing up? Are you proud to be Italian now?

I tried calling my grandpa's sister, Rose, his last living sibling. She lived in Washington state, and I rarely saw her growing up, but I knew she liked my mom, and I was hopeful she would want to talk to me.

It didn't go well. She was irritated with me and still felt disdain for her parents, siblings, and childhood. The call ended abruptly with her saying, "I know nothing of my family in Italy. Nothing."

I didn't give up. I still haven't. It's difficult to justify why I feel such a connection. Such a desire to know and to understand. But it's real and it's strong.

With my grandpa and his family gone, I have to use more traditional, and unfortunately less personal, genealogical resources. Birth records. Passenger manifests from ships. Books about southern Italy.

My favorite resources are the memoirs of other Italian immigrants. Especially those who immigrated to Helper, Utah like my ancestors. The Carbon County Historical Society published journals, sharing immigration and other life stories from the diverse population of people who came to work in the mines. I scoured the journals for stories of my family, to no avail. But I devour the stories of my childhood neighbors, knowing my family likely had similar experiences.

The ship manifesto of the Vincenzo Florio on May 7, 1901 shows my great-grandfather's misspelled name. Saverio Manelli. He was fifteen years old, and he traveled alone.

When I visited Ellis Island, I imagined him a lone traveler lost in the crowd, scared and quiet, the transcribers hardly able to understand him in the enormous room, filled with the commotion of hundreds of foreigners.

I interviewed a neighbor in Helper who knew him and described him as a "tough old billy goat." I imagine him bold and overconfident, having just traveled across the world by himself at a young age.

I think of the story my Grandma Marrelli told me about him, her father-in-law, playing with her children when he thought nobody was looking. "He had a rough exterior, but he was a softie inside." I imagine him silent but strong, being ushered in a crowd, hoping he's being pushed the right way.

But that's all I can do. Imagine. Piece together the few memories I've been able to record from those who knew him and guess what that meant for who he was at different points in his life.

Writing, journaling, written histories, all things I appreciated before, are now priceless in my search for connection to the experiences of my ancestors who didn't have the privilege of literacy.

I listen to The Italian American Podcast (IAP), and I'm jealous of the stories they tell of their parents and grandparents. They share traditions, religion, and things they have in common. They debate red sauce versus gravy and argue whether or not Italian food should be static or dynamic. The imposter syndrome is fierce at times. Especially when I think about my Grandma Marrelli's Prego spaghetti and our many trips to Olive Garden as a family.

Then there are the moments where I feel like a part of the IAP *paesani*.

They joke about the way all the Italians they know protect everything to make it last, and I think of my Grandpa Marrelli telling me not to use the blinker in my car because it will wear it out.

They share how rare meat was in southern Italy and how when they came to America, they felt like kings because they could have meat once a week instead of twice a year. They especially loved pig meat and raised pigs to slaughter. I think of the logs of pepperoni and salami in the crisper at my grandparents' house, free for the slicing.

They tell stories about Italian Americans avoiding the doctor at all costs, and I think of my grandpa, over age seventy and retired. He cut the tip of his middle finger almost entirely off in the swather while cutting hay. It was hanging by a small piece of skin. I'm told he used a few choice words, wrapped his finger (dangling part included) in his handkerchief, and jumped back on the swather to finish cutting the hay.

The more I hear them reminisce about growing up Italian American, the more I realize that although I don't have the things we usually associate with heritage—traditions, authentic food, or language—there are attitudes and beliefs born of the Italian American experience that I still hold inside me.

The desire I have to tough it out when I'm hurt instead of seeking medicine or doctors.

The attitude that was ingrained in me to "grab a shovel and get to work" if there's anything that's important enough to me.

The belief that karma and what I put into the world have a

way of coming back around.

The importance of family. The fact that we gather every Sunday for dinner. That we're loud and in each other's business, and we show up for each other when it's important.

Italy—its culture, its architecture, its history—it's universally valued now. It's sexy. A place to travel, to find culture, to find love. In my naivety, I assumed that was always the case. That Americans always thought of Italy, even southern Italy, as a desirable place with desirable people. Maybe that's why I so readily claimed it.

There's a much darker side of the early Italian American experience. It isn't nearly as fun to learn and is more difficult for me to relate to. The discrimination of the "wops" and "dagos" in America. The lynchings. The difference in the papers from Ellis Island that designated Italian immigrants as either Northerners or dark-skinned, illiterate Southerners. A different class of people.

I wonder if this is why my grandpa told us he didn't speak Italian. I was naive to believe him—his parents never spoke English.

I wonder if this is why he didn't pass on any traditions or preserve any recipes.

I wonder if this is why my Great Aunt Rose spoke harshly of her family, her childhood, and Italy.

When I ask my mom if she experienced any discrimination, she always answers with her characteristic positivity. "Well, we've never been the mainstream." Whatever that means.

I think of every childhood picture I've ever seen of my grandpa. He's usually wearing a sailor's outfit, and there's always an American flag in the forefront.

I think of his father, who proudly took the name Sam instead of Saverio. A name I thought had been forced on him, but later found was a choice.

I think of the military service of my grandpa, his brothers, and my great-grandpa. Between the five of them, they served in each great war for the United States. They claimed America. They fought for her. Proudly. They dropped all that would mark them as anything but American.

Assimilation is a double-edged sword. I feel both sides of it. With none of the olive skin that makes my younger sister racially ambiguous, I've gone my entire life looking white, registering as white, and receiving all the privileges that come with it. The benefits of assimilation. I think my ancestors would be happy. I think this is exactly why they came to America and what they wanted to give to their posterity.

I may not have known my great-grandpa Saverio. I may only be able to imagine what he was like and how difficult his life was. But the gratitude I feel for the sacrifices he made is powerful.

He came to the United States "to become a king," according to my grandpa. Instead, he found a job as a hard laborer, poverty, and discrimination. Possibly better in some ways, but an equally difficult life as the one he left back in the old country. If only he could see his posterity just three generations later. Would he think it was worth it?

As strong as my gratitude is the loss I feel. The other side of the sword. The loss of culture, of tradition, of language. The whitewashing of our family that has resulted in the imposter syndrome I feel when I attempt to claim my place in the Italian American *paesani*.

Terra in the Italian language refers to the earth. The pejorative term *terroni* is used against people of Southern Italian descent because of its relation to dirt and the peasant class. When I learned about the insult "terroni" on the IAP, and the fact that Southern Italians have turned it into a word of pride, I instantly felt belonging in it.

I am from the dirt. I am from poverty. I am from scrappy hard workers who clawed their way out. I am from a people who valued family so much they sacrificed all they knew to provide a better life for their family then and their posterity to come. I may not be a "king" as my great-grandfather hoped to become when he left his small Southern Italian village behind at age fifteen. But I have infinitely more possibilities open to me because of the sacrifices he made in a world where he saw very few of the benefits.

I've learned so much since first presenting "Italian Deviled Eggs" to my eighth-grade FACS class. Though much of what I've learned has shown me a picture of a people who are far different from me and the life I've lived, there are decisions, core values, and tiny nuggets of tradition that withstood the test of time. It's in those details I find belonging.

We are connected to our ancestors. An unbreakable chain that spans generations. I stand on the shoulders of those who came before me. And the decisions I make, the core values I uphold, will forge the path on which those who come after me will begin their journey.

I'M NOT SARAH

Gina G

Sitting in the school cafeteria, hunched over my meager sandwich of bread, lettuce, and cheese, I cursed my mom for once again spending the food money on her pill habit.

"Amanda!" Mark waved from the cafeteria door.

"Mark! Jen!" I scooted my lunch over to make room.

"Hey, girl!" Jen sat down next to me and unpacked her lunch. "Did you see her?"

I broke free of her grasp. "See who?"

"The new girl. She could be your twin." Mark plopped his backpack on the bench and pulled out a large sandwich, a bag of chips, some candy and granola bars, a box of crackers, two sodas, and an apple.

"You want some?" he asked, catching my glimpse, or maybe hearing my stomach rumble.

"No, thank you." Yes. My lunch sucked. I just didn't want to admit it. Pride. I'd dug through restaurant leftovers the night before just to come up with anything decent to eat. And where was my mom? Sacked out on the couch, high on whatever she'd taken earlier.

"Help yourself." Mark crunched on a chip. "So, the newbie's name is Sarah Empey. She's from California. Moved here over the Christmas break."

"Why?" I couldn't imagine anyone giving up California with its high-rise buildings, oceans, and wine country for the desert heat of southern Utah.

Jen leaned over the table and whispered, "Rumor has it, she was getting in trouble, so her family moved here."

"How would you know that?" Jen was the queen of gossip. She batted tarantula lashes innocently. "What? People tell me things."

"Who?"

She waved a hand at me. "I can't reveal my sources, you know that. But check it out, she just walked in."

I turned to the doorway and there she was. Sarah. She was my height and build, her hair a light brown shade compared to my dyed black locks. She was dressed in an olive-green sweater with jeans, Ugg boots, and a Coach handbag. Money. My lookalike had money. Figures. I wanted to hate her. She was talking to Lauren and Jeff, all smiles, hands clasping her books tight to her chest. I watched as she laughed at whatever they were saying and almost choked on my sandwich. Her laugh was like mine. My jaw dropped.

"See, she's your freakin twin." Jen nudged me.

Sarah turned her attention to the students in the cafeteria, caught me staring, and strolled over. She sat down across from me, scooting Mark over with barely a glance.

"Who are you?" she leaned across the table, scrunching her nose as she studied me.

"Amanda Burnett and you are?"

"Sarah Empey."

"Welcome to Dixie High," Mark said. Sarah didn't even glance at him.

"When's your birthday?" she asked.

"August fifteenth." Were we twins separated at birth?

"I'm September fifth."

"Close," I replied and had to ask, "Were you adopted?"

"No. You?"

"No."

"Uhm, hello ladies?" Mark tapped his smartwatch, "We have fifteen minutes till class."

Sarah's snapped her head to the left noticing him for the first time. She beamed a smile and held out her hand. "Hi, who are you?"

"Mark," he pointed a finger at Jen. "This is Jen, short for Jenna."

"Nice to meet you," Jen said.

"You too." Sarah turned her attention back to me. "What's your next class?"

Against my better judgment, we became friends.

Sarah's favorite color was purple, mine was maroon. We both loved tacos, chips, and cookie dough. She was interesting, in a weird sort of I-already-know-you way. We liked the same type of music, books, and movies. We had the same eyes, the same laugh, the same smile, and even the same mole behind our right ear. It was uncanny. After two weeks of getting to know each other, she invited me to her house for the weekend. I happily accepted. It wasn't a tough choice. Did I want to stay at my rundown apartment or go check out her four-bedroom, four-bath house with a swimming pool and game room? Seriously? Hands down her place.

"So your parents don't mind you staying over for the weekend?" she double-checked as we walked to the parking lot after school.

"Not at all." They couldn't care less, and probably wouldn't even notice I was gone.

Sarah unlocked her Jeep and we drove to her place. It was on Foremaster Ridge, white brick, with a view of the city from the back. A two-story with the main living, kitchen, and master suite on the first floor and the other bedrooms and game room on the second. The outside was fully fenced with landscaped gardens and a kidney-shaped swimming pool.

"This is a great place." I stood in the kitchen taking it all in.

"When it gets warmer, you can bring your swimsuit. Maybe we could invite your friends Jen and Mark."

"Maybe." My friends. Not sure if I wanted to share them just yet.

I followed her into the kitchen and watched her load a tray

with cheese, crackers, sausage, mustard, chips, and dip. "What would you like to drink?"

"Water is fine."

"There is some soda in the pantry." Sarah's mom stepped into the kitchen. She was a few inches taller, with nut-brown hair falling to her shoulders in a soft curtain. "Do you girls want anything else? Popcorn? Juice? Chocolate?"

"We got it, mom." Sarah rolled her eyes.

"Okay," her mother looked closely at me, studying me from behind her glasses. "You must be Amanda. Sarah said she had a twin friend."

"Mom."

"What? Can't I comment about anything?"

"Nice to meet you." Politeness had me holding out my hand.

"You too." Sarah's mom shook it. "I'll get out of your way."

"Thanks." Sarah grabbed at my arm, and we hurried upstairs to the game room. "Sorry about that," she said as she powered on the large screen TV dominating one wall. "My mom is so nosy. She is forever trying to control my life."

"Control?" The rumors Jen mentioned when Sarah arrived surfaced in my mind. "Why would she try to control you?"

Sarah let out a heavy sigh, her shoulders deflated. "I got into trouble a few times in California. We moved here to help me out."

"What kind of trouble?"

"The usual," She flicked on the TV and found a show to watch. "Drinking, drugs, hanging out with the wrong people. Normal teenage stuff, you know."

No, I didn't know. After watching my parents give in to their addictions, I did not want to be like them.

"So, my mom is always in my business."

Must be nice. I thought of my parents who couldn't care less about anything I did.

"You know," she reached for a lock of my hair and held it between her fingers. "If I dyed my hair black like yours and cut it, we would look exactly alike."

I didn't think so. "Your scar would set us apart."

"Easy fix." She dipped a piece of cauliflower into some ranch and bit into it. "We could use a knife."

"A knife!" I scooted back, eyes wide.

Sarah laughed, shaking her head at me. "A pocketknife, silly, or something small. It just has to match mine."

"How did you get the scar?"

"I fell off a swing when I was three." She replied, "What about you? Do you have any scars? Broken bones?"

Tilting my head to one side, I thought about it. "No, come to think of it, I don't."

"So, what do you say?"

"To a matching scar? Why?"

"Well . . . we could switch places, I could go to your classes, and you could go to mine."

"Interesting," my thoughts immediately went to my algebra class. I hated math. "What else could we do?"

"Only one way to find out." She waggled her eyebrows at me.

Switch places with Sarah? Tempting. The school would be one thing—what I wanted was her life. What would it be like to have a loving family? To have money? To be able to afford to do anything I wanted?

"Fine, let's do it." It was just a little scar.

Clapping her hands, Sarah ran into her bathroom, reappearing with a bottle of hydrogen peroxide, some band-aids, cotton balls, a pocketknife, and a lighter. She set those on the ottoman.

"One last thing." She held up a hand before disappearing downstairs. Moments later she returned with a bottle of vodka and two shot glasses. She filled one glass and handed it to me. "Here, take this. It'll help with the pain."

I didn't want to. But I also didn't want the knife to hurt. "Shit. Okay." One drink wouldn't kill me, right?

Sarah held up her shot glass, "A toast then, to twins. Kindred spirits. Partners."

"Friends." My hand shook as we clinked glasses.

Sarah downed her drink in one smooth practiced motion. I followed, tasting the burn, and a hint of candy flavoring before I coughed. Pouring another shot, Sarah dipped the blade into the liquid, pulled it out, and picked up the lighter, burning the blade clean. She handed me some cotton balls.

"Hold these above your eye, and let me know when you are ready."

I swallowed, biting my lip. Pressing close to me, she tilted my head back, her long hair tickling my cheek. "Ready?"

"Yes."

The next morning, we drove to the store and bought a box of black hair dye. We hit the mall next searching for similar outfits. The rest of our day was spent getting Sarah's hair to match mine and trying on clothes.

When we went down for dinner, her mother did a double take, and her father lowered his glasses. Sarah pirouetted in a circle and nodded to me. I did the same.

"What do you think?" I asked. We had rehearsed this upstairs, thinking, if we could fool them, we could fool anyone.

"Well, it's different." Her father remarked and went back to setting the table.

"Amanda," her mother glanced right at me, "do you like spaghetti?"

"How did you know?" Sarah huffed and sat dejectedly down in her seat.

"A mother knows," she replied.

"I hate spaghetti," Sarah said.

"I love it." Homemade spaghetti? Not frozen or served from a can? What wasn't to love?

"It's the scar," her mother said as she sat down. "Sarah's is old. Yours is still new."

It made sense. Mine was still angry and red. Sarah and I agreed after dinner we'd need to pull our hair over our scars to hide the newness of mine.

Monday, we showed up at school with our twin look, the same style of jeans, the same tee shirt, and the same shoes.

"Think it will work?" I asked when we parked.

"Only one way to find out," she said as we got out of her Jeep and walked inside.

"Remember," Sarah murmured, "You're me and I'm you."

"Got it, Amanda," I whispered back and opened the door.

We clasped pinkie fingers and stepped inside. People paused, giving us a double take, before moving on.

"Hey, Amanda," Jen rounded the corner, deeply concentrating on her phone.

"Yeah?" Sarah and I both said at the same time.

Jen looked up, eyes darting back and forth between us. "Wow, am I tripping?"

Sarah cast me a devilish look, this was it. "No," she pointed to me, "Sarah copied my hairdo. We wanted to see if we could fool anyone."

"It's freaky." She circled us, stopping in front of me. "Sarah, I don't know why you colored your hair, but it looks good."

"I'm Amanda." I stepped in front of Sarah.

"Right," Jen tapped Sarah on the shoulder and said, "Well, right now Amanda and I are late for algebra."

Sarah laughed our laugh, and they trotted down the hall to my class. It worked!

I went to Sarah's history class. No one in school suspected a thing. We thought it was funny, a joke, nothing serious. Or at least I did. Sarah had other plans.

A few weeks later, I was home studying, when a picture was posted on Instagram with the hashtag "#drinking games, #Amanda's night out, #just one more." It showed Sarah at a party with a bottle of vodka. What the hell? She was posing as me? At a freakin' party? I didn't like alcohol. I didn't want to be like my parents. What was she doing?

As I was reading the post and checking out the pictures, I got a text. "Amanda, I'm stuck in Cedar at a party. Can you go to my place, and tell my parents you're me? Please?"

"Fine."

I pushed myself away from the chair I was sitting in and

walked in a slow circle around the dining room table. What the hell was her game? She was posing as me in Cedar. Partying. Drinking. Ruining my reputation.

I put my hands on my hips and stood in my meager apartment. My mom was passed out drunk on the sofa; my dad was back in jail for a parole violation. No one gave a shit what happened to me. Heck, mom wouldn't even notice I was gone. I dug twenty dollars out of her stash and called an uber to pick me up and drop me off at Sarah's house.

Pushing the front door open, I paused when I heard the sound of her parents arguing in the main room.

"She's doing it again, Rick." Her mother sounded on edge. "I can't go through it The partying. Drinking. Drugs!"

"Now, Lily, we don't know that. Stop jumping to conclusions."

"But, Rick, she's not here, she's not answering her phone." The sound of pacing.

I thought about closing the door and going back.

"We can't control her," Rick said. He added something else, but his voice was too low to make out what it was.

"I'm so done with this," Lily started to cry. "I wish I'd never given birth to her."

"Lily, you don't mean that. She's our daughter. She's just going through a phase."

I couldn't take it anymore. I coughed from the doorway and called out, "Hello? Mom? Dad? Sorry, I'm late. Mark, Amanda's friend, dropped me off. The Jeep was having issues."

I walked into the main room with a fake smile. Lily was wiping her eyes clear. Rick unwrapped his arms from her and gave me the briefest of nods.

"What happened with the Jeep?"

"Think the battery is dead."

"Why don't I drive you back and we can check it out," Rick suggested heading towards the coat closet.

"No, dad, Mark said he would check it in the morning. Not a problem. I'm starving—did you have dinner already?"

Lily still hadn't spoken. She just watched me from behind the sofa. I didn't think I was fooling her. Biting the corner of my lip I walked over to her and hugged her. "I'm so sorry, mom. I should have called, but I didn't want to worry you."

She leaned back and stroked my hair with one hand. "It's okay. We had spaghetti for dinner. Let me make you a plate."

"Let me help."

For the first time, I experienced a family night.

Sunday, Sarah returned, and I went back to my unwelcome home. Everyone acted as if nothing happened.

"You are ruining my reputation," I hissed Monday morning, my arms folded across my chest as I confronted her.

"Oh, stop it." She gave me a half hug. "Just look at it this way. You are finally having some fun."

"It's not the kind of fun I want to have."

"Oh, lighten up." She rolled her eyes.

"Hey, Amanda." Josh Warton, the school quarterback came around the corner. "I had a lot of fun Saturday night with you. Say we do it again this weekend?"

"No," my voice was firm.

"Oh, Sarah, stop it. He wasn't asking you." Sarah smirked and gave me a wink.

Josh looked me over. "Well, since there's two of you, why don't you join us . . . double the pleasure you know?"

I stomped my foot and stormed off. I didn't know what to do. To make matters worse, even Mark and Jen believed I was partying. They'd seen the pictures. Hell, Jen was at the party—she watched Sarah as me knock back drinks and shots.

"I thought you weren't into that?" she asked me at lunch.

"I'm not."

"Oh, right, Amanda is. You're not Amanda, you're Sarah."

I wanted to hit myself, to do something, anything, but our past few weeks of switching places had everyone confused. No one knew who was who, and Sarah kept pretending to be me, getting me in trouble with the school, me in trouble with friends, and me facing a bleak future of ruin while her parents plotted to send her away to college. It wasn't fair, and no matter how I shouted and pleaded and told everyone it was Sarah not me, no one believed what I was saying.

What's that old saying? Actions speak louder than words. Well, Sarah's actions as me yelled volumes.

My Saturday nights were now spent at her parent's house pretending to be her, getting to know Lily and Rick, and acting like the daughter I believed they deserved. The type of daughter I wished I could be with my parents.

But I was getting tired of the charade.

A week before graduation, I was at Sarah's house getting ready to go to the senior party at the convention center. We were in her bathroom primping.

Sarah was fixing her hair in a wild teased style reminiscent of the eighties. I kept mine simpler, going for straight sleek locks.

"We should look the same," she pushed her lower lip out pouting.

"We do," I applied dark plum lipstick and handed it to her. "Only our hairstyle is different." We were wearing matching jeans, shoes, and tank tops.

"Come on, Amanda, it's the senior party."

"I'm tired of trading places, I'm tired of everyone thinking I'm this wild party girl when I'm not. Why can't we go as who we are?"

"One last time?" She clasped her hands in front of her, begging. "Please, I promise."

"Swear to God?"

"Yeah, I have to stop anyway because it's almost summer, and you know my parents. . . . What college are they sending me off to?"

"Snows, up north."

She took my hands. "Look, I know I've been acting all crazy for the last month, but, I just needed to get some of the wildness out. Now I have to knuckle down and be the good girl, and I have you to thank for that. You saved me, Amanda. You came here week after week and pretended to be me. It can't have been easy."

It was. "No," I lied, "It was hard at times. For one thing, I wanted to hang out with my friends. This is my town you know. I grew up here. People know me. And now they know a side that isn't me. They already judge me because of my parents, and you've made it easier for them to believe that. I'm going to have to spend the entire summer pretending to be in rehab just to get my reputation back."

"One more night," she begged, "I promise not to drink a lot."

"Swear?"

"Swear."

"Okay, fine," I rolled my eyes. We slicked her hair back to match mine.

"Here," she held her phone out. "Let's take a selfie before we go." And she snapped a picture, tagging me.

"If I'm driving, I'll need your ID and everything."

"Of course," we traded wallets and phones before heading downstairs, stopping to say goodnight to her parents.

"Be back by one, girls." Her mom enveloped me in a hug, adding, "Stay safe and have fun, Sarah."

"Thanks, mom. Love you." She smelled like lilac and sandalwood.

It was raining outside, thick drops drenching the heat-soaked ground. I held my hands out and leaned my head back feeling the blessed wetness soak into my skin. Sarah grabbed me, squealing, and pushed me towards her Jeep. Laughing, we started it up and drove to Mark's house first before hitting Jen's.

The convention center was decorated in Dixie High's blue and white colors. A paper mâché biplane hung from the ceiling, floating between silver-dangled stars. A table sat to the far right, loaded with fruit punch and snacks. Mark produced a flask with rum in it. We spiked our drinks between dancing, crowded in front of the selfie station, and had our pictures taken. The four of us, my two best friends and Sarah, my kindred twin.

"Thank you," she whispered in my ear, as we stumbled to

our table, sitting heavily down.

"For what?" I asked reaching for the half-empty glass of juice I'd been drinking earlier.

"For letting me into your life." She hugged me. "I've never had close friends before."

I gave her a light push and waggled my finger at her. "Now, Amanda," I emphasized my name. "Don't get sloshy drunk on me. You promised, remember?"

Her eyes swam in giggles. "I remember."

Mark and Jen returned from the dance floor. Jen raised an arm to her forehead and closed her eyes, leaning her head back.

"I am so tired, you guys." She blew out a breath.

Mark glanced at his phone. "Yeah, it's getting late. We should probably head home. You ladies ready?"

I stretched, looking over at Sarah who stretched with me.

"God, you two are like mirror images, unless I'm seeing double." He held up his flask.

"Put that away," Jen batted his arm down. "We don't want to get caught."

"All right, let's go." I stood up and offered Sarah a hand. "Come on, Amanda."

Outside the skies were dark with clouds, and the air was a chilly snake wrapping around me. Rain fell in a constant splatter, and we ran for the Jeep covering our heads. I unlocked the doors, and we all piled in. The windows were misted over with moisture. I found the defrost button, and we sat for a minute letting the car warm up.

"You sure you're okay to drive?" Jen asked from the backseat.

"Fine." I'd only drank one cup with rum in it. I backed out of the parking lot and started for Jen's place first.

"Let me sip from that flask, Mark." Sarah, as me, held her hand out. Mark passed the flask over.

"Amanda . . ." I hissed.

"What?" she tipped the flask back.

I reached for the flask, and the Jeep swerved, skidding in the rain. Headlights flared in the window. I yanked on the wheel, and we spun. Jen screamed from the back, Mark cried out, the flask went flying, and Sarah swore. I grabbed at the wheel trying to remember to turn into the skid when we were hit. Metal screeched and bent, the Jeep crumpled, and I banged into the driver's door, shoulder jerked back by the seatbelt. The airbag exploded, white powder, the sound of glass breaking, shards flying, and my head whipped forward hitting the bag, smacking back, impacting, and everything went dark.

Sirens, noise, flashing lights, red, blue, rain. Everything hurt. I tasted blood and heard crying in the back, but who? I tried to move, and the world faded, swam, and spun in a wheel of color. The door was jerked open, and hands were reaching for me, the sky crying tears on my skin, my face.

"Are you okay, miss?"

I threw up. My eyes closed, a heavy curtain came down, and I faded, fell, and heard cries of "get the medics over here now."

"Sarah?" a voice brought me back, cool hands on my forehead. "Sarah . . ."

"Ma'am, are you sure?"

"You think I don't know my daughter?" It was Sarah's mom. She was holding my hand, stroking my hair back from my face.

"I'm not . . ." I tried to gather my strength. I could hear Mark off to one side, see a strobe flash of him wrapped in a blanket, and talking to an officer.

". . . it came out of nowhere and hit us."

"You're okay, Sarah," Lily soothed, and I looked into her eyes. She was crying.

"Amanda . . ." my name is Amanda, I wanted to say, but the words wouldn't croak out.

"Oh, Sarah, I'm so sorry. Amanda is dead."

"No . . ."

I'm not dead. I'm right here, and I remembered the ID switch, I remembered being behind the wheel of Sarah's Jeep, driving, the impact, on her side. My hands grasped at Lily's, held tight, "I'm . . ."

"It's okay, baby." She smoothed my hair back. "You're okay.

We're going to get you to the hospital and then home."

Home. My mom was drugged out, stoned, drunk, not caring what I did or where I went. My dad was in jail. They weren't here. Sarah's mom was here.

I could have her life. No one would know.

We had the same blood type, look, dress style, hair, and eye color. We could be twins.

I'm not Sarah.

But I could be.

I would be.

I was.

"Mom . . ." I sealed the deal and held her close.

A WICKED KILT

Amanda Hill

On a rainy afternoon, as I sat on wet asphalt in a pencil skirt and a broken stiletto, a man who looked like Thor's stunt double appeared out of nowhere.

I was running from my car to the theater, hoping to avoid getting soaked. It would have been easier if I'd had an umbrella, but instead, I held my purse above my perfectly curled hair to keep it from frizzing.

I should have taken the rain as a sign not to come. Curt and I bought tickets to this play months ago before we broke up and both of us being here was a testament to how stubborn we were. Neither of us was willing to let our ticket go to the other. It had little to do with money and more to do with the fact Wicked came around only so often in Salt Lake City. And maybe also because I couldn't let Curt win.

I could handle a night sitting next to my ex for the opportunity to see Elphaba fly.

A tiny hole in the asphalt had been my undoing, catching my heel just right—or wrong. But now that my clothes were soaked through, and my purse lay in a puddle a few feet away, the dumb decision of showing up was as clear as the droplets running down my face.

It might as well have been a brick wall standing between me and the doors to the warm theater. But I didn't want to give up and go back home either, so I sat. Like I was sitting on a park bench on a sunny spring day in May.

That's when Thor's stunt double showed up. His hair wasn't quite as long, but it was blonde with a tighter curl, framing a face so perfect it belonged on screen.

While I could tell his body had the muscle definition to match Thor, he chose to wear a baggy brown sweater over a green-plaid kilt with baggy sweats peeking out underneath. Why he would try to hide such a beautiful figure, I had no idea.

He had to have come from the theater. Maybe they were practicing some sort of Scottish play? Except Eccles Theater didn't produce plays. They only hosted traveling shows, and even if they did, I doubt they'd let someone wear a costume out in this rain.

He was just as surprised to see me as I was to see him. A couple of cars on either side and dark clouds kept me hidden to anyone who wasn't ten feet in front of me.

He stopped, took a step back, and tipped his head to get a better look at me.

It wasn't every day you ran into a professionally dressed woman watching rivulets of rain pool in the pavement.

"Can I help you?"

His voice was as deep as I expected, though it didn't sound like Thor's. He didn't even have a Scottish accent like his outfit might suggest. Just regular old American, but rich. Rich as in robust, not the money kind of rich. A scruffy beard and the outfit gave the impression he wasn't rolling in cash.

"Did you know if you can meditate in the rain, you can meditate anywhere?" I'd never actually heard that before, but it sounded ridiculous which meant it was probably a creed on some website or social media post somewhere on the internet. I thought it would make me sound like I knew what I was doing, but instead made me sound like a fugitive from a mental hospital.

Judging by the look of his kilt, we might have escaped from the same place.

"And you are interrupting my meditating," I said as the rain continued to soak us. As bad as it sounded, I was committed and might as well take it all the way.

You're welcome hot-stranger-in-a-kilt for giving you the excuse you were looking for to bolt and never come back.

But he didn't take it. Instead, he held out his hand. "I'll help you to your car."

I can't say I was shocked he didn't believe my meditation story. I considered the hand stretched out to me. Large and rough by the looks of it. Familiar with hard work. Did they farm in Scotland? Oh wait, he didn't have a Scottish accent.

Taking his hand was the only logical solution since I'd decided not to go forward or back. At a point in my life where I didn't like the two options before me, he'd offered a third, and I couldn't turn that down.

His hand was as wet as mine, but warmer.

After another slip where I would have fallen without his forearm supporting the small of my back, I decided not to let that hand go.

"You sure you have your balance?" he asked.

If I said I didn't, would he keep me close?

Too soon. We barely knew each other. I stepped back.

"Yes." I forced the muscles in my legs to stop flopping and reluctantly let our hands slip out of each other's grasp. "Why are you wearing a kilt?" Best to turn the attention on him.

"It seemed like the right choice to make this morning." He gestured to my fancy clothes as he picked up my soiled purse from the ground. "Much like choosing to wear formal attire while meditating in the rain."

Touché.

He hadn't asked to escort me to the theater, even though that was the direction I'd been facing. He must have known that was my destination. Did he assume I would want to leave after a fall like that? After getting soaked in the rain? What if I still wanted to see Gah-Linda?

"Actually, I have tickets for the play," I said, turning to face the theater, which although a terrible idea soaked as I was, seemed much more attainable now I was on my feet. I'd dry eventually.

"You sure you want to go?"

"You think I shouldn't?" The reasons I shouldn't go were obvious, but it wasn't for him to decide.

He paused like he was about to argue but thought better of it. "Then I'll escort you to the theater." He held his elbow out for me like he was a gentleman in 19th century England and I was a lady. Did they have the same rules of etiquette in Scotland? Oh, that's right, not from Scotland.

"Are you from Scotland?" I couldn't help it.

"The Scots aren't the only ones who wear kilts. The Irish do too."

"Are you Irish?" One that maybe speaks with a fake American accent.

"I think I have Irish ancestors." He expertly avoided my vague inquiries on his choice of clothing. But then again, I wasn't going to tell him why I was so determined to see the show.

This would actually be better. Curt would be so mad having to sit next to me looking like a wet rat. Mad enough he might even leave. Maybe I could invite kilt-man to take his place, and we could be wet watching a show together. It was always easier when you could be an idiot with someone else.

Bright lights shone in rays from the glass doors ahead of us, illuminating the well-dressed theatergoers inside. With borrowed light from the chandeliers inside, I looked down at my soaked outfit and nearly had a panic attack. How could I have forgotten I had on a white, button-down shirt?

Using my arms to cover the bra that was no longer hidden underneath, I faced kilt-man with a mix of shock and horror. "Why didn't you tell me?"

Before he could answer, I turned and ran back down the steps.

Not a good idea with one broken stiletto over rain-soaked cement, which I should have already learned. But stumbling, I made it to the bottom without falling. The faster I could get away from light, the better. I'd have to go home, find a pint of ice cream, and settle in to watch Hamilton on Netflix.

He appeared in front of me again, standing in my way.

"I offered to walk you to your car."

"And I said no." I kept my arms folded over my chest attempting to regain some dignity.

I never actually said no, but now I was.

He didn't look anywhere but my eyes, which he'd been doing the entire time we'd known each other, despite having plenty of other things to look at. I might have realized the state of my clothing sooner if he'd stared. Maybe I'd been too quick to blame him.

"I don't have to walk you to your car. I just offered because I didn't think you'd want to go back to the theater, and you looked like you needed help."

Knowing I'd needed his help didn't make it any easier.

"I should have been more direct," he said. "I just didn't know what to say."

Did I expect him to point out my see-through shirt? It wasn't his fault I fell and got soaked in the rain.

But I could make it to my car on my own, and I was about to tell him as much, when he took off his kilt.

"Here," he said as he held it out to me.

"You think I want that?" What would I do with a wet kilt recently wrapped around a stranger's waist?

He chuckled, and the sound it produced rolled and tumbled around in my head while his smile accentuated the dimples on his cheeks.

I momentarily forgot what we were talking about.

"It's clean, I promise. Just wet."

Before I could argue more, he threw it around my neck, and the gesture was oddly intimate.

"See. Now it's a fall poncho."

The kilt was thick and waterproof. Despite the water on its surface, the inside was dry and warm.

Now he wore only a mismatched sweatsuit, and I was the

one who looked Scottish. Or Irish. Or whatever. Did women wear kilts?

"Now you can go to Wicked." He said it with a straight face, but at the slightest hint of a smile from me, we both broke into laughter.

"You don't look as ridiculous as you think. You really pull that off."

He was just saying it to be nice. Even if the kilt was the right color to pull out the green in my eyes, my hair was plastered to my face and my makeup had to be running down my chin.

"I'll go in if you join me and say hello to everyone we meet in a Scottish accent."

"I don't have a ticket."

"Leave that up to me." I had no plan, but it seemed the right thing to say.

He cocked an eyebrow. "Who says I can speak in an Irish accent?"

"I said Scottish."

In a perfect Irish accent, he replied, "Most people can't tell the difference anyway."

I laughed, and he held out his elbow for me again. This time I took it with confidence and stepped up to the doors like we owned them.

The ticket agents only checked the tickets visually because the theater was sold out. If anyone tried to fake tickets, it would be clear when two people tried to occupy the same seat. Curt was probably already in his seat—he was always early—and when we ran into him, kilt-guy would have to leave.

"Hello," he said in an Irish accent to the first person who widened their eyes at the sight of us. "Top o' the morning to ya."

I didn't know what I thought would happen. Maybe I wanted Curt to see me with someone as hot as kilt-guy, or maybe I enjoyed the way the man in the wet sweatsuit made me forget to be uptight and have a little fun.

The general public either snickered or obviously avoided

looking at us, and before long, gave us a wide berth.

At first, I was so embarrassed I kept my gaze on the floor, but hot guy didn't seem to be affected by what everyone else thought.

How could he not care? We'd chosen to break the rules of fashion, personal hygiene, and general compliance, and the price for such behavior was embarrassment. Everyone had to pay.

After one particularly stellar performance from kilt-man, I picked my gaze up from the floor and watched him. Did he always have this much confidence?

"What is your name?" I whispered. It hadn't come up before, but I wanted it now. More than I wanted to see Scarecrow choose Elphaba over Glinda. She had always been the one for him.

"Adam."

He whispered it without an accent. Like a secret he would keep from everyone else in the theater but me. To all the people around us, and for my sake, he'd put on an act, but to me, he was the gentleman who'd shared his kilt and forged the way to my seat so I could see the show I'd been anticipating for months.

A show that I somehow had less desire to see now, even though I could never get enough of Popular.

What would happen when we got to my seat and Curt was there? Adam would have to leave, and I'd be stuck in a wet kilt with the man who couldn't be bothered to do anything for a relationship, let alone give me a kilt when I needed it.

I would rather be ridiculed in a public square with a guy like Adam than fit in with Curt and everyone else in this stuffy theater.

The next time Adam gave someone a "top o' the morning" I joined in, though my accent was so bad it shattered the effect—Adam didn't seem to care. He only smiled wider.

Whether he was following my lead to the back door, or we both knew we would never actually make it to the seats, we ended up back outside in the rain.

"What's your name?" he asked.

"Anna."

Adam hadn't changed the rain, but he changed the way I saw it.

Adam Honstein never lost. He could beat the house in Vegas or win a ping-pong tournament at the office—he only had to decide it was worth the effort.

But Samantha had changed all that. She'd come along with witty candor, an infectious laugh, and a wealth of philosophical ideas they could discuss for hours. It didn't hurt she was a ten.

He should have wondered why she would pick him. It wasn't that he had a hard time attracting women, he just always seemed to attract the wrong kind, and Samantha was everything right.

At least he'd thought.

It took him a long time to realize what she'd done. She'd used his competitive spirit against him, turning everything into a competition she made sure he won. A sophisticated version of reverse psychology.

When she had him stuck in her clutches, she changed gears, making good sense suggestions impossible to argue with. Her lease had run out, and it made sense to move in together, it didn't mean anything in the relationship, it was more like roommates, but you knew what you were getting into.

Then she found great investment deals but hid them. At least, that's how it had seemed. Looking back, he could see how she planned for him to find them.

When he did, she begged his forgiveness, spinning a story of promises she'd made to keep quiet, the opportunity was for only a select few.

She'd wanted to tell him, of course, but she was too honorable to break a promise. And to make it up to him, she would invest his money under her name and give him back what his money earned.

Now that he was outside her control, the deception was so obvious, but it hadn't been then. It killed him that he had somehow become one of the idiots that fell for scams like that.

He helped her out with her car payment when she was in between jobs, picked up her morning coffees from the local coffee shop, and paid for most of the groceries. She kept him feeling like he was lucky to be with her.

It took losing his life savings in the investment to wake him up. He hadn't told anyone he'd invested with her, and he vowed he would never tell anyone how stupid he'd been.

Samantha hadn't been home when he realized the truth and broke free from her grip. He was smart enough to know if she had a chance to speak, she'd convince him to stay with her.

Instead, he boxed up everything she owned and put the boxes outside the front door to greet her when she returned.

He wanted to be gone by the time she returned, but she showed up as soon as he finished.

She did everything he expected, laying on the charm, but he'd wised up. When she realized she couldn't get through to him anymore, she flipped in an instant.

It was like the transformation from the Queen to the old hag. Instead of honey-flavored flattery, she dropped her cloak of civility and threw insults at him until she lost her breath.

None of it changed anything.

After she'd left, taking her belongings, she called and texted him incessantly until he had to block her number.

A few days after he blocked her, she showed up at his door.

"My kilt is still somewhere in here, and I want it back."

It wasn't late, but it was dark, and since he wasn't going anywhere, he'd put on the only clean, comfy outfit he had—a mismatched sweat suit—and planned to catch up on the latest season of the Blacklist.

"It's not your kilt."

"You bought it for me at that vintage store."

"I bought it for me."

When she'd lived with him, they visited a local vintage shop and came across a kilt that looked just like the one Axl Rose wore during one of his concerts. They decided then and there to dress up like Guns N' Roses though they hadn't decided who would be whom, and everything fell apart soon after.

"You can't tell me you're going to wear it," she said.

He left her at the door, fetching the kilt from his closet. He should have put it in one of her boxes—he didn't want it—but in all the packing, he'd missed it somehow. The only thing he'd missed.

She was right, he would never wear it, he didn't even like it, but because she wanted it, he'd never give it to her.

He came back to the door with the kilt around his waist and told her to leave.

"It's meant to be worn outside. That doesn't count."

She knew he was particular about his clothes. He didn't usually like to dress up, even for Halloween, because he didn't want to look dumb. But she'd done that without changing his clothes.

He didn't have to listen to her anymore. He could wear the kilt inside if he wanted to.

He closed the door in her face and went back to the television.

She knocked a few times and yelled something he couldn't understand with the steel door between them, but he ignored her.

When the yelling stopped, he got up to be sure she was gone.

It had started raining.

The rain mesmerized him, and he had the sudden urge to step into it. One step led to another, and as he walked, he let the pain of the past few months wash away as the drops first soaked his hair, then his clothes, and finally his skin.

Except where he wore the kilt. That was waterproof.

He wasn't doing it to prove to Samantha that the kilt was his, or even to ruin it, which he thought migh happen. Except the kilt was waterproof so maybe it was meant to be worn in the rain. He had no idea how to care for a kilt.

He did it because it wasn't like him to walk in outside in the rain, especially dressed like this. And it bothered him that Sam knew how to get to him. He had a weakness, and she'd exploited it.

He didn't want to have weaknesses others could use on him.

Maybe that was part of the reason he'd come out in the rain, though he hadn't known it when he left. If he could face the attention of strangers and the odd looks they threw his way—and there were more than a few—maybe he could be strong enough to overcome what Samantha had put him through. And walk away from who he'd been.

Eccles theater drew him in. The bright lights and the sparkling patrons. He didn't want to get close enough to make a scene, but he wanted to get close enough to feel some of the atmosphere. Maybe when he'd recovered financially, he would treat himself to a ticket. Even if he sat alone.

He stopped when he ran into a woman sitting on the ground, more wet than he was. She needed help, but he didn't know what to do.

He said something, and she said something back.

Looking back, he never could remember just what they'd said to each other, but the conversation flowed, and he found himself inside the theater pretending to be Irish while the strange woman wore the kilt like a cape. She looked much better in it than Samantha ever would have.

He'd never tried an Irish accent before, but he was pretty good. Who knew?

When he walked out the back door with her, he wasn't thinking about Samantha or how embarrassed she'd made him feel. He thought only about this woman on his arm and how she helped him forget, if only for a few minutes.

It turned out he was the one who needed help.

And she had come to the rescue.

A CHRISTMAS MEMORY

Pat Partridge

None of them had family who would be visiting on Christmas Day.

I was going to be alone too. My sons were visiting their mom whom they hadn't seen since the summer. My stepsons had plans with their dad. My current wife was with her boyfriend. Months earlier she'd announced she had fallen in love and moved out.

Clearly, it made sense that I would be alone, if sense is the right word.

Normally, I can handle being alone. But Christmas was going to be hard. I pretended it didn't matter that I'd be by myself in the normally kid-noisy house—I'd have complete control of the remote! But it didn't work. Sadness has weight, and when Christmas was only a few days away, I could foretell the impending crush of loneliness.

I looked inward and decided to reach outward. Whom could I help who would also be alone, stranded by circumstances beyond their control?

I contacted nursing homes in my area, spoke to the directors, and asked a single question—Do you have residents who are going to be alone on Christmas Day who might appreciate a visit from a stranger? Two nursing homes accepted my offer.

On Christmas Eve I stopped into a nearby Safeway with an unusual request—Do you have flowers I could give to nursing home residents who will be alone on Christmas? Take as many as you need, the flower lady said. I took a dozen red roses, four per person I planned to visit. She also gave me three small vases to hold them and bunches of baby's breath, a flower that symbolizes both innocence and everlasting love.

My first stop on Christmas day was the Life Care Center not far from my home. Mary Ellen, eighty-three, her family away visiting relatives, was the first person on my list.

I walked down to Mary Ellen's modest room. She was sitting up in her elevated bed, sound asleep. She looked frail, but her white hair had been curled gracefully by the staff. A bedside table held a two-foot-tall artificial Christmas tree and two Christmas cards propped on their edges. The curtains were partially pulled, but sunshine sent a slash of light across the foot of the bed.

I sat quietly in the Naugahyde-covered chair with its stainless-steel armrests and waited. I felt awkward and worried she'd startle when she awoke and saw me sitting there; my good intentions would be wasted if I upset someone I wanted to cheer up. But as I sat, her steady breathing and calm expression eased my anxiousness, and my breath slowed, matching hers.

When fifteen peaceful minutes passed and Mary Ellen didn't awaken, I arose quietly and placed the vase with its four red roses on the bedside table. Maybe I'll come back after visiting Rose, I thought.

The manager had offered a gentle warning—Rose might not respond well to a stranger calling on her. I was about to find out. I walked to Rose's room, several doors down from Mary Ellen's room. Rose was definitely awake. She sat propped up in bed, an afghan over her lap, intently watching Miracle on 34th Street on the tv hanging on the opposite wall.

"You must be Pat," she said as I stood in her doorway. "The staff said I was going to have a visitor." She was blunt, not smiling.

"Yes, that's me," I said. "May I come in?"

"Sure." She motioned for me to have a seat.

Rose, eighty-five, had a soft, round face, her white hair thinner than Mary Ellen's. Her skin was a robust pink, her eyes blue and clear.

"Why are you here?" she asked. She seemed more curious than angry.

"To spend time with residents who don't have family visiting for Christmas. That's all."

"Well, my daughter and her husband and their three kids stopped by last week before they went on their big ski trip. They all wore Santa hats. Made me wear one, too, for a group picture."

She laughed, almost a snort. "You could see the guilt on their faces, like I was going to kick the bucket while they played in the snow. But I liked the Christmas cookies they brought. And I'm wearing the new robe they gave me." She fingered the lapel. "A clean robe is about as fancy as we get around here."

"It looks nice."

She shrugged. "Yeah, well, I must have a dozen of 'em."

I nodded, unsure how to respond. I still held the vase in my lap.

"These are for you," I said, placing the flowers on her bedside table.

"So, you're playing good Samaritan," she said when I returned to my seat. She nodded gently and her voice softened. "You alone today too?"

"You could say that."

"Got any kids?"

"Three boys. They're out of town with their mom." I didn't mention stepsons. Seemed it would complicate things, lead to more questions about their mom I didn't want to answer.

"I see," she said.

I didn't disagree. That she couldn't really see the depth of the hole in my heart was okay with me.

We talked. Ten years earlier she'd moved to town from Oklahoma to be closer to her daughter and grandkids. Her husband, Frank, had been alive then. She asked if I played bridge and said "that's too bad" when I said "no."

"Now I have diabetes and kidney issues and need help getting to the bathroom. That is, if I make it."

I asked if she needed to go, and she laughed.

"I'd be pushing this here button if I did!" She indicated a call button that hung from the bed. "And you wouldn't want to be around!"

I took the hint and didn't ask why.

We talked some more. But Rose kept glancing at the tv. She'd turned down the volume when I sat, but the movie drew her attention away from me. The iconic courtroom scene where Kris Kringle proves he's Santa Claus had come on. She wanted to watch, not talk to me.

That's okay, I told myself, I'm not here for me.

In hindsight, I'm sure if I'd said that out loud, Rose would have roared.

"I must've seen this movie a thousand times," she said. "But I like the old classics, don't you?"

"That one, yes," I said.

I stood.

"Want to watch it with me?" she asked, as she turned up the volume.

I smiled. "Maybe some other time. But you know how it is for good Samaritans. Always rushing around. I've got one more visit to make across town."

She laughed again. It was a strong, throaty laugh I hoped she'd still have a decade on, a laugh that felt like a present for me.

She called out as I reached the doorway. "Hey, Pat!" I turned.

"Thanks for the flowers. Roses are my favorite."

"I thought they might be."

"Merry Christmas," she said.

I stopped by Mary Ellen's room. She still slept soundly. The scent of the roses had gently permeated the air. I took a small card out of my pocket to place next to the flower vase. "Merry Christmas," I wrote, and signed it, "Kris Kringle."

The Serenity Senior Care Center was my next stop, a one-story complex on the outskirts of town. Across from its parking lot, three horses in a small field, blithely unaware of the holiday, munched on the sparse grass. Beyond them new houses were under construction, their spindly wooden frames looking like tinker toys, but the hammers were quiet on Christmas Day. Soon an entire neighborhood would rise where bare fields had been; someday, the horses would be gone too.

Eventually everything changes, I thought.

Over the years I'd learned the painful life lesson that things which seemed solid—were solid, even—could crumble into dust. Or worse, into quicksand. I'd learned the lesson, but the shock of losing something precious still hurt—a spear to the soul.

Helen lived on "the memory care wing." Entering or leaving the wing was only possible if you knew the code. The residents of the wing didn't know it and couldn't remember it if told.

The manager on duty walked me to Helen's spartan room. (It reminded me of my first college dorm room before my roommate and I covered the walls with posters we were sure made us look cool.)

A small painting hung on a wall—a guardian angel hovering over a child. A sky-blue blanket covered a single bed, and a handful of well-worn magazines lay stacked in a small bookshelf. Helen sat calmly in a corduroy-covered lounge chair.

She had a beautiful, innocent smile that brightened the moment I arrived at her open door. Later, I realized it reminded me of my grandmother's smile in her last years. To this day, I think the serenity of both their smiles came from having no obligations to make others happy, not even an obligation to make oneself happy.

"Helen, you have a visitor," the manager said. Helen rose from the chair slowly but gracefully, apparently without discomfort or pain.

"Hi, Helen. My name is Pat. You don't know me, but I've come to spend some time with you on Christmas day." I held out my hand, and she took it. I tried to match her gentle grasp with my own.

"That's nice," she said. "When is Christmas?"

The manager spoke up. "It's today, Helen. We're going to have a party in a little while." She turned to me. "Can you stay for the party?"

"Sure. I have plenty of time." I fought the temptation to brood about the seemingly vast time alone I still faced. I thought, What good is feeling sorry for myself? But that didn't stop me from feeling sorry for myself.

A fact sheet the nursing home gave me told me a little about Helen: She was eighty-two. She'd never married and had no children. One of her siblings, a sister, was still alive but couldn't visit. Helen had been in the memory care wing for six months and had advanced Alzheimer's, which meant that, unless she needed hospitalization, this was where she would die. Alone, I thought.

There was one fact about Helen that surprised me and connected us—she'd been a college professor (I never learned which subject) at the university in my hometown.

I sat on the edge of the bed, and Helen and I talked for a while, an awkward but sweet conversation that didn't seem anchored to any reality—hers or mine. I asked about her past, but she didn't remember my hometown. Or being a professor. Or her family.

It was my first experience with someone with advanced Alzheimer's. Later, our exchange made me think of two teenagers on their first dance date, trying to find something to say and not step on each other's feet. Helen and I fumbled and searched for what to say too, but still we talked. And smiled. And that seemed good enough for both of us.

When one of the aides announced the Christmas party was about to start, I escorted Helen to the small kitchen and dining area where the residents of the memory wing ate, separated from the main dining room.

A six-foot tall Christmas tree, decorated with simple paper

ornaments, likely made earlier by the residents, stood in one corner, a green plastic garland hung above the kitchen cabinets, and tiny snow-flocked trees or Santas stood in the middle of each of the tables where the residents ate. Three staff members, all women, one wearing a Santa cap, jovially greeted each person, helping some with their wheelchairs, others with getting comfortably seated. They likely were foregoing precious time with their own children and grandchildren, but the warmth of their affection radiated like the Star of Bethlehem.

It was the most wonderful Christmas setting I'd ever experienced.

Helen and I sat along the wall at a small two-person table, a six-inch Frosty the Snowman for company. We watched the staff prepare the party treats—a sheet cake cut into small squares loaded onto paper Christmas plates, orange juice in holiday cups, and tiny cups filled with green and red M&Ms.

Helen smiled brightly. "Now, who are you?"

"I'm Pat," I said. "Your new friend."

"Oh. That's nice."

I don't think my name mattered, but she still understood what having a friend meant. As we talked, simple, childlike topics seemed best. For both of us. "How's your cake?" I asked.

"Good."

The sense of taste diminishes with age, I knew, but the primal allure of sweetness stays strong, and the room quieted as the residents ate their treats. Soon the staff put a CD into a small boombox on the counter.

"Ready to sing?" said the aide in the Santa hat.

Some nodded quietly, still eating; others said "yes" with fervor.

"White Christmas," the original Bing Crosby version, played first. The residents sang along, stumbling over the verses until Bing crooned the chorus, "I'm dreaming of a white Christmas." Everyone joined in with, "just like the one I used to know." Helen and me, too.

"Jingle Bells" followed. Everyone sang, "Jingle bells, jingle bells, jingle all the way" with the enthusiasm of a kindergarten class, and faces lit up. Helen's too.

I marveled that this group of seniors could recall—with cheery gusto—songs they'd learned seventy, even eighty years earlier, although few could remember the names of the staff, or the names of their own spouses and children.

Memories matter. Or do they? We hold some memories so close to our hearts we believe they define us, give our lives meaning. Yet . . . here was a group of seniors whose unconscious memories of childhood songs—sung with joy—were the ones that remained unscathed. Other memories were simply gone.

Should I feel sad for their loss of memory? I struggled with the question. They'd lived long lives—working, raising families, worrying, laughing, crying, loving others. In short, making memories. Even though those memories were no longer available to them, their lives had been rich. Maybe that was enough.

That's when I realized, I have a long life ahead in which to create new memories.

The singing ended with "We Wish You a Merry Christmas." When we all sang, "and a happy new year," I choked up. Many of these wonderful people would not finish the next year alive. And yet at that moment, they were happy.

I suspect Helen didn't remember me the next day. That's okay. I remember her.

THOSE WHO HAUNT THE NIGHT

C. H. Lindsay

'Neath sun and moon
And stars too bright,
We hide from that
Which haunts the night.

Yet with our songs
And tales of plight
We summon woes
To haunt the night.

For money, fame,
And to give fright,
We write those tales
That haunt the night.

And in the end,
It's pure delight
To be the ones
Who haunt the night.

THE HAMMER CLUB

Johnny Worthen

Ms. Kosminski's note to meet her after school would be the kicker for an already perfectly terrible day. Not that today was different from any other day.

The note had found him in Math, where Mr. Pendleton called him to his desk and then, loudly, said "Ms. Kosminski wishes to see you after school." The whole class heard and smirked. Mr. Pendleton too. Accusation and joy that the school dweeb was about to suffer. Again.

When the bell rang, Andrew waited for the classroom to empty. No hurry to get to the bus now. At least he would be spared the trouble of rushing for a seat. No one would share one with him otherwise. Mr. Pendleton ordered him out after only a few moments, while the halls were still full of the little monsters who'd made Andrew's life so miserable.

Carrying his backpack in front of him like a shield, he moved against the flow of students toward the English classroom, the note crumbled in his fist, wet with sweat and anger of the injustice about to be imposed on him.

Again.

But not for long. He had a plan and a rope and soon . . .

The room was empty and smelled like air freshener. He went to his usual desk, sat down, and instinctively flinched imagining Bryston slapping the back of his head. That happened every day in English, at least once, and in the hall if Andrew didn't see him in time. In other classes they shared, Andrew had managed to sit away from the bully. But in English, he hadn't been able to get away from him.

"Mr. Johnson, I'm glad you came," said Ms. Kosminski coming in from a side door. "I hope it wasn't inconvenient for you."

It was. He'd missed his bus, his mom wouldn't be home for hours so he'd have to walk home. It'd take an hour and it was cold out. "Not a problem," he said.

Ms. Kosminski locked the door to the hall.

"I want to talk to you," she said.

"What about?"

Ms. Kosminski was old for a teacher, probably in her forties. Teachers were usually young and didn't last long at Springview High. Half the teachers he'd had in his freshman year weren't there now for his sophomore.

She watched him—studied him—as if looking for something beneath his skin.

He looked at her as if for the first time, noting, consciously, the gray roots under her brown hair, her boxy glasses, plain beige blouse and cardigan, slacks and flat shoes. She had a gold chain around her neck but no rings.

"I want to talk to you about Bryston," she said.

He didn't answer.

"How long has he been bullying you?"

Andrew shrugged. He knew now where this was going. He'd been down this road before, gone for help in the vice principal's office only to be told to lump it and try to make friends.

"He's been at you all year," said Ms. Kosminski. "From the first day. He chose to sit behind you, I think, for the explicit reason to torment you."

"He's just an ass," Andrew mumbled.

"I know he lives only a couple streets from you. You ride the same bus?"

"Yes."

"Were you in junior high together?"

"Yes. And Grass Lane Elementary."

"Has he always . . . been an ass?"

Andrew shrugged.

"I noticed last month you had a bruise over your eye and blood on your collar. What happened?"

Andrew shrugged again. Ms. Kosminski kept him in her stare.

"He punched me on the bus."

"Did the bus driver see it?"

"Yes." Why lie?

"What happened?"

"I got cleaned up and went to my classes."

"Does that kind of thing happen a lot?"

"Sometimes."

"Do others bother you too?" She moved forward and sat herself on his desktop.

"He has a gang, but he's the worst."

"I know what you're going through," she said.

He had to roll his eyes, and he blushed when he realized that she'd seen him do it.

"Kids picked on me all through school," she said. "All the way from Green Lane Elementary through Manor Creek Middle to Springview High. The same path you're on."

"Manor Creek sucked."

"And Springview High sucks too, doesn't it?"

Andrew shrugged. "My father said that school was just something to endure," Andrew told her. "'Get through it,' he said. 'It'll get better.'"

"I haven't met your father."

"He left when I was eleven. No idea where he went. Cleaned out the bank and was gone."

"Just you and your mom now?"

"She brings home guys sometimes."

"Yeah?"

"Got a bruise or two to show for that too."

Ms. Kosminski nodded in understanding.

Andrew rolled his eyes again. "Can I go?"

"Not just yet," she said. "Have you talked to the counselors?"

"And the vice principal last year. Same story. 'Boys will be boys.' I swear he gets off on it."

Ms. Kosminkski nodded in agreement. Andrew didn't know what to think.

"Girls are just as mean," she said. "Worse sometimes. Cruel bitches."

He'd never heard a teacher swear before. He knew the word, but it didn't sound right coming from Ms. Kosminkski

"Bullies and monsters are everywhere and always," she said.

"So it doesn't get better?"

"Not without some assertion."

"Make friends?"

"No. Quite the opposite."

"Fight them? I'd get my ass kicked."

Ms. Kosminski drew her hand up to her neck and played with the thin gold chain. "When I was in school, my problem was Lisa Blamire. A real piece of work. She had blonde hair and perfect teeth and her parents had money. From day one, she hated me and made every day of my life as bad as she could."

"Did counselors help you?"

Ms. Kosminski laughed. "No, Andrew. No, they didn't."

"Vice principal? Teachers?"

"No and yes."

"Ah, okay," he said. "What happened?"

"I was a sophomore, like you. Mr. Richards taught Social Science, down in the E hallway where math is now."

"I know it."

"He told me that wounds that are picked at never heal. Scabs that are ripped open can only scar and scars are forever."

"Wow," said Andrew. "How deep."

Ms. Kosminski smiled. "I knew there was fight in you."

He shrugged.

"I wasn't the one picking on my wound, and if it went on, beyond the time when I could deal with it, it would never heal."

"What was it?"

"Me. My self-esteem."

"Okay."

"People like Lisa and Bryston are everywhere. They're toxic their whole lives."

"Once out of here he'll be out of my hair. He brags that his dad can get him into Harvard."

"For his father's money," she said. "His grades surely won't get him there."

"He got a new car," said Andrew. "A Mustang. It's all he talks about."

"And yet he rides the bus?"

"I think just to torment me, but it's probably because he's afraid to bring his car to school."

"Smart. Too easy for you to key it."

"I hadn't thought of that."

"Yes, you have," she said. "And you've thought of worse."

"What are you getting at?"

"I did Lisa myself. I only needed a little inspiration. I had nothing to lose. She had a car too. Hers was a little Volkswagon bug. Cute little thing. Red. She had a little kaleidoscope crystal hanging from the mirror."

"Bryston has fuzzy dice. If that's not cliché, I don't know what is."

"I dropped a note in her locker. I signed it her boyfriend's name. Jerry Edwards. Another piece of shit. They'd been meeting out by the bleachers for weeks playing tonsil hockey and stretched sweaters, so it wasn't suspicious when she got a note suggesting another meeting. Jerry was gone. Went home early that day sick. His chicken fried steak didn't agree with him. He threw up for a week."

"Okay…"

"Did I mention I worked in the lunchroom?"

"No."

"Well, I did."

"And?"

"And?"

"And what happened."

"I met Lisa behind the bleachers."

"What did you do?"

"What do you think I did?"

"Egged her car? Punched her in the nose? Poured blood on her?"

"I cracked her head open with a ball-peen hammer," she said. "Mr. Richards stole it for me from shop class. It was never missed."

Andrew's head was spinning. The mood was calm, the setting mundane, but the words and deeds they described were alien and misplaced.

"Was she okay?" he asked.

"Oh, no, Andrew. She was not. She was dead as disco. Dead dead dead."

Andrew looked into her face to find the joke, but it wasn't there. His teacher smiled warmly, affectionately even, better than any counselor had ever done for him.

"And?"

"And, we put her in her car, drove up to the top of 8th Street—you know the really steep one?"

"I know it. It's a dangerous hill."

"We put her in the driver's seat, released the gears, and down she went into a telephone pole."

Andrew shook his head, feeling the motion to wake himself, not believing, not understanding.

"The school went into mourning for a month. 'Poor popular Lisa, taken too soon, victim of a standard transmission and over-eagerness.'" The words were spoken in baby-talk, lisped sibilants and condescension.

"Did no one . . ."

"No one," she said. "I was free. I've been free ever since."

"You're scaring me."

"Don't be scared," she said. "Let me finish my story."

"Okay."

"I became a teacher and came back here to Springview. My alma mater. I've been here for twenty-two years."

"That's a long time. How could you stand it?"

"I keep it interesting by finding students like me, like you, Andrew. Outsiders who just want to be left alone, to be given time, but who are harassed by bullies. 'Bully' is of course a kind appellation. They're maggots, a blight on society, the worst of us."

"They get better," he said. "It gets better." It was his mantra until he found the courage to use the rope.

"No, they don't," she said. "There's no reason for them to change. I give them until sophomore year. If they haven't turned the corner by then, there's no hope."

"Whoa . . ."

"Jeff Malhem needed my help first. He was well before your time. Margorie Pajala after that. Gareth Gray and Amy Nelson. Amy's just two years ahead of you. Do you remember her brother Scott?"

"Scott Nelson? Yeah, he died in a swimming accident last year."

Ms. Kosminski smiled. "No. We killed him," she said. "In this very room."

Andrew shuddered. His mouth went dry. He leaned back in his chair, making what distance he could without alarm.

"I didn't do anything," he said, tears welling.

"Of course you didn't." She put her hand on his. It was warm and caressing. "But you have to. If you don't, you'll never get over it. The wounds will fester and scab and then scar."

"But . . ."

There was a knock on the door. Ms. Kosminski got up and went to it.

Andrew thought of running then, busting out a window, running to the office, telling someone—a counselor, the vice principal, anyone—but he hesitated. Nothing good had ever come from that direction and what would he say? Who would believe him? He didn't believe it himself.

This classroom was not warm to him, never welcoming. In fact, he'd hated this class not for Ms. Kosminski but for Bryston, he reasoned. Ms. Kosminski had called out the bully when she'd seen something. At least she used to, at first. Not lately though. Not lately.

"I really should—" he began.

Bryston stumbled through the door. He was wrapped up in cellophane, like a leftover. His arms and torso and face were all beneath layers of clear plastic. Andrew could see a brown sock stuck in his mouth under the prismatic layers.

Four people came in with him, ages over the spectrum from just graduated to old.

Ms. Kosminski said, "Andrew, I'd like to introduce you to Jeff Malhem, Margorie Pajala, Gareth Gray, and Amy Nelson."

"Hi, Andrew," said Amy, waving.

"We're glad we can help you, son," said the oldest one, Jeff, Andrew assumed.

"His car?" asked Ms. Kosminski.

"We have it up on 8th," said Marjorie. "Ready to go."

"It's a dangerous hill," she said.

Bryston wiggled and fought. The one who must be Gareth kicked him in the back of the legs, and he fell to his knees.

Amy peeled the wrap from the bully's eyes. He looked around terrified and panicked. His gaze fell on Andrew and held there.

Ms. Kosminski went to her desk, opened a drawer, and removed a ball-peen hammer. She held it out to Andrew.

Andrew looked at Bryston, read in his face the realization that he himself had just come to.

"Best thing you'll ever do, son," said Jeff.

"It's like taking all their power to yourself," said Marjorie. "It'll over-double what you are now."

"There's no hope for this one," said Amy. "Bad seeds cannot grow true plants. The world will be so much better without this dirt."

"What if I don't . . ." he began.

"Don't want to?" said Ms. Kosminski, "then you'll be lying."

"What if I don't do it?" he said.

"We'll cross that bridge when we come to it," she said.

He tried to read a threat there, to feel pressure—greater pressure, true duress to do the thing, but he felt nothing. Around him were sympathetic eyes, faces who knew the pain he'd endured all his life, people who'd shared the unending terror of creeps like Bryston.

Andrew found himself standing, felt himself shuffling toward Ms. Kosminski's desk. "There are people like this everywhere," he said. "I can't . . . them all."

"You won't need to," said Gareth. "Probably."

"They're everywhere, to be sure," said Ms. Kosminski. "They walk among us, but we also walk among them."

"Focused and properly directed rage," said Jeff.

"It's surgical," said Graham, "Better than an indiscriminate AR-15 at lunchtime."

"Or a rope at home," added Ms. Kosminski.

Andrew stared at his teacher, who offered him only the most loving comforting smile. Around her, the others did the same, some faces he'd seen before, not many, but all of them he recognized.

"And we'll be there to help," said Marjorie, "if you can't manage it alone."

They all shared a look together that sent a chill down Andrew's back.

"Has anyone ever . . . refused?" he asked, taking the hammer into his outstretched hand.

"No."

Slowly, deliberately, as if in a dream coming true, Andrew turned to face the bound bully Bryston, who wiggled and fought and beseeched with his eyes, right up until the end.

THE COLLECTION

Talysa Sainz

The knife sunk into my chest for the sixth time, and I lost consciousness.

When I awoke, I was lying on the floor, and my whole body felt full of sharp tingles, as if all my circulation had stopped. Marked was scrubbing the floor next to me, whispering, "What have I done?"

I scrambled away from him, afraid he would continue the shocking assault, but he didn't even notice that I had moved. He also didn't seem to notice the collection of people standing around us. I scurried to the closest person, a portly, jolly man in pin-striped suit pants and suspenders.

"Help me!" I called. "My husband is trying to kill me!" But nobody moved. I tried to get the attention of one woman near me, but I stopped when I saw what looked like dried blood all over her arms. That's when I realized everyone around me looked like they were in the middle of dying—bullet holes, blood stains, even rope burns across the neck. A woman dressed in what looked like an old Victorian costume came forward.

"Maggie. Welcome to the afterlife," she said.

What did she mean? I backed up. "How do you know my name? Who are you?"

Suddenly afraid these strange people in my home were not friendly, I ran to the front door, swung it open, and attempted to throw myself outside.

But I couldn't move.

The Victorian-looking woman came up and pulled me back, with much more strength than I would have thought she had.

"I'm Lady Cora," she said, as if I hadn't run away in the middle of our conversation. "I'm here to help you." I looked her up and down and realized she wasn't wearing a costume but actual Victorian clothing. Why on earth would she be here, in my home?

Something about the woman was extremely unnerving. Everyone seemed to follow this woman with their eyes without ever meeting her gaze. Nobody else was speaking. Nobody seemed to care that my husband had tried to kill me and was still in the room. Something about the whole situation was unnerving.

"What's going on?" I asked.

Lady Cora gripped my arm and escorted me back to the living room. At least twenty people filled the room, all as pale as Lady Cora and looking as nervous as I felt. The only one making any noise was Mark, still scrubbing the floor, next to...

Next to my body, clearly dead.

The police didn't come for several days. Weeks before Mark was arrested. Months before the house was put up for sale. It all happened exactly like Lady Cora said it would.

I sat on the sofa. My pile of books on the shelf was gathering dust. What good was the afterlife if I couldn't spend my time reading?

John, the portly, friendly-looking man I had first run into after I died, noticed my melancholy and came and sat on the couch next to me. John was probably the least threatening person here. He apparently drank himself to death, so nothing about his appearance showed a gory death. He had dark circles around his eyes, but those weren't out of place for a ghost anyway. I had constant stab wounds and blood soaking through my shirt, as pale as everything else about me. Sure, it was dry now, or did it count as dry if it was ethereal? I wasn't sure.

Nobody asked how Lady died. Or maybe they had, but no one talked about it. Rumors circulated, of course. She once said she wanted a big family, so maybe she died during childbirth? Except she wore an extremely nice dress, and there was no blood on her person. Nobody really knew.

"I'm so bored," I shared.

"It gets easier," he said. "Think of it like retirement. No more work, no bills to pay, and all the time in the world."

"But I liked my work. And I liked my life." So maybe that last part was a bit of a lie. Depression liked to rear its head at the most inconvenient of times.

John put his hand on my shoulder and gave a soft squeeze. "It'll get easier," he promised.

"Why am I here?"

He let go. "Your husband was a very jealous man."

I waved off his answer. I had never cheated on my husband, despite his ramblings moments before he killed me.

"No, I mean, why am I here. Of all places. Shouldn't there be some sort of . . . place for us to go? Not everyone gets stuck eternally wherever they died, right? Why are we stuck here? There must be some way to move on."

His face dropped to his lap. "We've tried, dear. Lord knows we've tried. Lady has been here longer than anyone, and she tried for several lonely years to 'move on' somewhere better, just to be disappointed over and over again. I don't know why we are here, but at least we're not alone."

He stood up and left me to my thoughts.

I moved to the end of the couch, where I could read the pages of the book I had left open the morning before the argument with Mark. I had read the same page again and again. I was starting to lose my memory of what had happened before, and the curiosity of what came next was killing me. Or, it would if I wasn't already dead. I concentrated so hard—it was so frustrating—I put all of my energy on the book, until the pages fluttered just a bit.

A small squeal escaped my mouth. I tried again, willing all my concentration on the book, imagining the page moving.

A page fluttered up and down. I stood up and clapped my

hands.

"Lady Cora!"

Lady Cora must have been close because she appeared in the doorway almost instantly.

"I swear, Lady, I just got a page of my book to move! I concentrated on it, and the page moved. I know you said we couldn't move objects, but—"

But Lady Cora did not appear happy about the revelation. She was downright furious.

"Do you even hear yourself? Thinking you can suddenly move objects, as if all of us haven't been trying for decades. It's preposterous." She sighed, took my hand, and pulled me to sit on the couch with her. "You all go through this, you know. Every one of you. But I warned you, didn't I? I warned you, and if you dwell on this, it will drive you mad. You don't want to end up like Eddie, do you?"

A shudder raced through me. I didn't want to go mad.

Lady Cora patted my hand, stood up, and left.

Eddie lived in the basement. If this place had been filled with people rather than spirits, Eddie would be the ghost story we told each other in whispers. A few days in, I heard one of his tantrums. He was throwing things against the wall and yelling something about "that bitch" who had murdered him. Lady Cora told me she keeps him downstairs because he is dangerous. Rumors circulated that he went crazy trying to move things, trying to escape this house. Lady Cora went down and visits with him occasionally, but she didn't trust anyone else.

Except Grace.

Grace was the wife of John—they actually met and got married here, in the afterlife. They were very cute together and often talked of how they would have raised their children had they met while living. Grace was Lady Cora's helper, and she did what she did was told. She didn't seem to have a lot of fire in her. But I did.

Did Eddie try to move things too? Did he ever succeed? Did it really drive him mad? I needed to find out. I walked to the basement door, made sure nobody could see me, and opened it.

I had never believed my house was haunted. My agent warned me when I bought the house that a fair amount of people had died in the house. But I never gave much credit to the idea of a house being haunted, or there being bad luck about a place. The house was pretty, well-kept, and the price was well within our price range. And the stories of the house drove away most prospective buyers—either because they feared the supernatural, or they just didn't want to be the ones living in the Murder House. I didn't mind. We moved in, greeted the neighbors, and told them that if anyone could break the curse, it would be me.

But even before I died, the basement gave me chills. The temperature seemed to drop whenever I opened the door.

So whatever I expected of Eddie, it wasn't this.

He dressed in a suit, an older one for sure, but I couldn't place the date. He could be as old as Lady Cora for all I knew. The room was set up like a Victorian tea party—how did I never notice that when I was alive?

"Eddie?"

Eddie turned around, looking irritated. His mouth grimaced as his eyes flashed to mine.

"Come to gawk?" he asked. "I admit, you ventured down here sooner than most." Eddie held a book and set it down as he turned his body toward her.

"How did you do that?" I asked.

He waved me off. "We should at least do this properly," he said and gestured for me to sit down. I crossed the room slowly, keeping a close eye on him, before sitting down in a dusty chair. An awkward silence filled the room.

Eddie appraised me up and down, studying, then turned his attention to the teacup sitting in front of him.

"So . . . how long have you been here, Eddie?"

"A little over a century."

"Wow! You must be the longest living resident." Eddie snorted, but I continued. "You probably know more about Lady

Cora than anyone."

"That much is true," he admitted.

I didn't want to push my luck, but my curiosity got the better of me. "Do you know how Lady Cora ended up here?" Maybe if I knew how the first resident got stuck, I could figure out how to undo it all.

Eddie set down the teacup, put his hands together, and studied her for a moment before answering. "Cora hired someone to bewitch the house to keep the souls of those who died here forever. She then poisoned the man she loved. But even in death, he could not love her back. Eventually she tried to kill another man, but the spirit of her first victim switched the teacups, and Cora accidentally poisoned herself. The man, or ghost, thought that if she died, her spell would die with her and he would be free, but he was wrong. The spell was neither cast on her nor cast on him—the spell was on the house itself."

"How do you know all of this?"

Eddie picked up the teacup once again. "That is a story for another time." He turned the cup over in his palm.

"How . . . How do you do that?"

He sighed in annoyance. "Just concentrate," he said. "It's not that difficult."

And then I asked the question I was most afraid to ask.

"Why does Lady Cora say we can't move objects? Do we really . . . do we really go mad when we start doing that?"

Eddie leaned forward, keeping his eyes locked with mine. "Do you think I'm mad?"

"Well, honestly, no. You seem strange enough, but we're all ghosts, so everyone and everything is strange to me right now. You don't seem dangerous."

"I'm sure Lady Cora would disagree with you."

"I don't really care."

For the first time, Eddie smiled, and he looked at me like he was really seeing me. How many times had the residents of this house come down to investigate Eddie, and how many of them left with the same opinion of him that Lady Cora had told them to have—that moving objects had made him go mad and dangerous? What was so scary about him that she would try to make people afraid of him?

Before I left, I stopped and looked into his eyes. "Well, it was nice to meet you, Eddie." I turned around and started walking up the stairs.

"It's Edward," he said.

I smiled. "Edward," I said, instead of goodbye.

I walked up to my old room. It was Lady Cora's now—she got the owner's suite. Not that she slept. She just liked having her own space, and it must be important for her to have the biggest one. I lingered by the door. How many times had I felt a cold chill go through me while I was sitting in bed with my laptop, watching TV, or folding laundry? It was creepy. Lady Cora had been living—well, dwelling—in my room the whole time I lived here. Why did she get to rule this place? It wasn't fair. And it was time someone did something about it.

"Maggie!" I startled as someone behind me said my name. It was Lady Cora. "What do you think you are doing?"

"I just . . . missed the view from my old window. I was hoping the door was open so I could see through it again," I lied. Lady Cora glided past me. Glided? Was that the right word? Most of the ghosts had taken to gliding now that they could. I still liked to walk. So did Edward, I reminded myself. Lady Cora glided the way an old Victorian ghost would. But this wasn't that. This time it was forceful. As if she had been marching past, but without moving her legs. It gave me the creeps.

Lady Cora stopped right in front of me. "There must be order in a woman's household, and I maintain that order. You would do well to remember that," she said. It felt like a threat. Lady Cora backed off a little. "The new family is moving in tomorrow. And I want all of us to be on our best behavior. This family deserves a happy life here, and we will do all we can to make that happen for them."

The next day, the new family showed up. The parents were a young couple with two adorable little kids—a boy of five and a girl of seven.

Before I knew it, weeks had passed. Time moved differently when you were dead. When you aren't acting like you're living, you hardly remember what you are doing.

One day, Lady Cora asked for help. "The parents will be gone at a party, you see, and I'm worried that Eddie will act up in their absence. Would you be a dear and spend some time downstairs with him while they are gone?"

I could tell Lady Cora was full of shit about Edward's attitude, but I wasn't going to turn down the chance to spend time with him without having to sneak down there. Lady Cora didn't know I had been practicing moving things with Edward in the basement. I had started with my book and moved on to bigger and bigger objects.

But when I got to the basement door, something felt off. Extra cold. I looked around, wondering where Lady Cora was and why she wasn't going downstairs herself. I noticed the stove was on—extra weird. Then I noticed the children lying down on the floor in the kitchen. I rushed to them to make sure they were okay. They weren't playing. They weren't breathing.

I looked around for help, but the room was empty. Odd, for this time of day. "Help! Everybody, come help!" The collection of ghosts slowly peaked out of doorways, congregating at the entrances to the room without fully entering it. "You have to help me get them out!"

But nobody moved. They just stared.

John came over, put his hand on my back, and said, "Just let them be."

I shook him off. "What are you talking about? We have to get them out of the house. This is gas poisoning, and they are dying."

"They will be safe," he said. "We will take care of them."

"But they deserve life! This is not life; this is death." I pulled away from John and started pulling the little girl by the arm, but I couldn't get a good grip on her. Somehow, I needed to wake them up. With a groan, I thought of the babysitter, probably passed out somewhere too.

"Step away from her, Maggie." Lady Cora had entered the room. She stood three steps up on the staircase, just taller than everyone else. She spoke with calm authority, like she did the day I died.

"You did this. I know you did. You can't keep us all here. You can't treat us like your puppets. You try to create the perfect family for you, but nobody here loves you. They are all afraid of you. And no one deserves to be here."

I could feel the anger rolling off of Lady Cora, and so could the entire house—windows shook, curtains swayed, even the chimney sounded like it had the air knocked out of it. But I didn't back down.

"You killed all of us, didn't you? You got stuck here, and you didn't want to be alone. You're keeping us here."

"And what are you going to do about it? Nothing can bring you back to life. You are trapped in this house, just like the rest of us."

I stood up. "You're right. But you can't have the kids!"

"Oh, it's too late for them." A wicked smile spread across her face. This had been planned for ages, I realized—since the moment Lady Cora knew the parents would be out of the house for long enough.

It didn't matter what Lady Cora said. I would get these kids out of this house. Even if they died, they would not be stuck here with us.

I crouched down and concentrated on the little girl until I could lift the girl's hand into my own.

Lady Cora reached down and yanked my hand away. I couldn't do this without help.

"Please, help me." I turned to John. "We need to save these children." But he just looked at his feet and then at his wife.

"Now Grace can finally have the children she always wanted," Lady Cora said, as if it were the most benevolent thing in the world.

Of course. Grace had always wanted children.

"Anybody, please," I begged. The residents slowly disappeared through the doorways, back to their corners of the house. Was everyone really content to let these children die?

Grace stepped forward. Oh no. Would she have to fight through Grace too? What about John? Would they all stop me, assuming I could gather the strength to lift these children out?

But Grace stepped between me and Lady Cora and turned to face the old woman. "I want my children to have life, not death." And Grace lowered herself and asked, "Now how do we get them out of here?"

"You need to concentrate. It . . . takes practice. But just try. We have to try."

"We'll get the door," John said, gesturing to a couple other men to back him up.

I managed to pull the little girl three feet before Lady Cora shook the house again. The front door locked. The windows locked. The door to the kitchen closed and locked.

"No one is leaving. I am running this house, not you!"

I knew what I had to do. And only one person could help me. I let myself stop concentrating completely. So much so that I was no longer standing on the floor but floating just above it. And then I let go of myself and sunk into the floor. Lady Cora tried to grab me and stop me, but Edward pulled on my legs and helped me into the basement.

"What on earth are you doing?" he asked.

"We have to get the kids out. Cora is killing them." There wasn't much time—Cora was coming for them through the basement door.

"But no one can leave. Not once they . . ." he trailed off. "Are they still alive?"

"I don't see their ghosts around, so they must be."

He nodded, and we both ran. Up the stairs, around Lady Cora, and each to one of the children. We dragged the children toward the front door, but before we could get there, Lady Cora blocked our way.

That's when the residents surged forward and surrounded

Lady Cora, shuffling her to the side. Edward opened the front door and we tried to drag the kids out, but whatever spell kept us here was strong enough to keep us from even going outside.

How could we get the children out if we couldn't get out ourselves? The house was cursed. The house . . .

The house had to die.

"Edward, help me."

Whether or not he understood what I was asking, I couldn't be sure, but either way, he followed me as I ran off to the kitchen.

I opened a drawer and rifled through it until I held a box of matches. I opened it and gave a handful to each of us.

"It's a gas leak," I reminded him. "To poison the kids."

He instantly understood what I was asking of him.

Cora stormed through the kitchen door, finally having made her way through her collection of prisoners.

"You ungrateful bitch," she shouted. "I gave you eternal life, and this is how you repay me? I got you away from that dud of a husband, and I gave you a family, one you have never had."

I struck a match, but it did nothing. Lady Cora flicked her wrist, and the matches flew out of my hands.

Lady Cora backed me up against the wall and slapped me.

I stood my ground. "You lonely, pathetic—"

Lady Cora slapped me again. "I gave you heaven, but I can make your life hell," she warned.

"I doubt heaven is a prison," I said. "And if it is, I'll burn that to the ground too."

My eyes met Edward's just as he struck a match, igniting the kitchen in flames. "It's time to die, Cora, for good this time," he said through the fire.

"No!" she shouted. But it was too late.

I shoved Lady Cora aside and ran to the children in front of the door. I needed the curse on the house to break before the spirits were all freed and disappeared or moved on or whatever it was that would happen next. I didn't care what happened to me. I just needed to get through that front door with the children before it happened.

Edward was one step behind me. Together we lifted the children and carried them to the front lawn. My grip kept slipping, and my hand would slide through the little girl's shoulders. "You'll be okay," I whispered to them, my voice shaking as I prayed my assurances were true." I was disappearing. With a pang, I remembered the babysitter, but it was too late for her.

The fire worked. The house was dying, and the curse was breaking. They would all be free.

AIDEEN

Edward Matthews

I

Jake had planned to spend the summer before his Junior year passing time with YouTube and playing video games with his few friends. Then his father told him he was going to stay with his uncle outside of New Harmony, smack in the middle of nowhere. But what did it matter, he thought, it wasn't just school where he was mostly ignored.

Jake's uncle welcomed him, shaking his hand with awkward formality, and pointing him toward his room for the summer. He was worried when his uncle said he was going to be staying in the attic and eyed the pull-down stairs at the end of the hall suspiciously. But climbing the stairs, he found a large room furnished with a single bed with a standing lamp next to it, a wardrobe, and a chest of drawers. A desk and chair sat below the window. He liked it. A big space apart from the world and all his own.

That night he lay awake staring into the dark, thinking about how he could survive a summer with no Wi-Fi and non-existent cell service, before realizing that he was no longer actually looking into darkness. Shapes emerged in a way that was not simply his eyes becoming accustomed to the dark. Looking around the room, he realized that there was a dim light shining through the small window above the desk. It was pale, not like the street lights he was used to in the city, but duller, almost gray.

He got up, slipped on his shorts and t-shirt discarded next to his bed, and went to the window. He saw dim light emanating from a tree about twenty yards from the back porch. He could not understand where the light was coming from, but could clearly see the tangled silhouette of branches which were a stark contrast to the lush leaves of the trees he had seen along the road today. In the bloom of early summer, these were green and full of life. This tree, with its dull, foreign light, appeared dead and barren. Jake's curiosity was piqued. He had never been particularly adventuresome, but neither was he easily frightened.

He made his way as quietly as possible down the pull-down stairs, through the house, and into the backyard. Walking across the yard, he immediately saw the dead light emanating from a tangle of leafless branches. Drawing nearer, he saw the light coming from a small treehouse nestled in the middle of the tree. A ladder rose from its base to a trap door in the middle of the floor.

He tested the ladder to be sure it was not rotted or broken and, after finding it secure, he ascended. At the top he pushed on the trap door which easily gave way, swinging up and landing noisily on the floor of the treehouse. Jake emerged into pitch black, although he was sure he had seen a light from the window. He raised himself into the space, keeping his feet on the ladder. As his eyes became accustomed to the dark, shapes began to emerge.

There was no furniture. No chairs to sit on for secret club meetings. No makeshift desk to look at childhood treasure maps. But in one corner, there was a shape like a pile of rags or clothing. He stared, straining in the darkness to see what this was, not moving from his perch at the top of the ladder, not yet committed to fully entering the dark space.

The lump moved. The pile shifted.

He started, leaning back but maintaining his grip on the ladder. He thought that he heard a faint sound like insect wings vibrating, but then silence. Jake steadied himself with the thought that his mind had been playing tricks on him in the dark. He was in a new place, tired and anxious from the trip. That was it.

Then a stench hit him and sent his mind reeling to burning rubber and hair. He bolted down the ladder and into the house, crossing the yard without seeing the blur of his surroundings. In the house, he darted up the stairs to his room. There he lay in the dark with his heart pounding, no more dull gray light shining through the window.

II

He awoke the next day with sunlight filling his room. The experience of the previous night on his mind, but less vivid. He dressed, ate breakfast with his uncle in silence, then nearly sprinted to the backyard. In the daylight, he found a normal yard. About thirty feet from the porch was a lone tree and the treehouse. It was not so barren as it had looked to him in the night. There were leaves, but they were smaller and sparser than those on the trees that lined the perimeter.

Though apprehensive, remembering the experience last night, the light of day emboldened him. He climbed the ladder and threw open the trap door emerging into empty space. The shadows he had seen the night before were nothing but phantoms of his imagination. There were no piles or rags littering the floor. There were no shadows, nor sounds, nor smells. No specters.

There were window openings cut into the walls on all four sides, open to the world. There was no way a smell would be trapped in here, and there was nothing to produce it anyway. He laughed at himself, climbing the rest of the way up, sitting on the floor and surveying his surroundings. There were no shapes or sounds or smells. It was a treehouse. No specters.

He sat for some time looking around at the tight space, feeling the breeze coming through the windows. Eventually, feeling bored, he made his way to the lawn.

As he landed on the grass he saw movement toward the woods beyond the yard. He caught sight of a figure, a girl he thought, moving quickly away from him.

"Hello?" he yelled.

He had not meant to scare her. But she did not respond, and she disappeared into the woods.

III

His uncle said very little to him, even when they were together at meals. Jake thought he probably didn't know how to talk to kids and was nervous. Most of the conversation consisted of one-line questions and responses like "What grade are you in?" or "Do you like school?" In his defense, adults usually don't know much more to ask about other than school.

But one night at dinner, his uncle looked him square in the eye and said, "I seen you out there by the woods every day. You ever see anything strange out there?"

"No," Jake answered. "I haven't seen anything weird in the woods." He wasn't about to tell him about the glowing treehouse. His uncle would think he was crazy and ship him off to some other relative for the rest of the summer or lock him in his attic room or something. "What . . . what would I see?"

"Those woods go on a hundred miles and then some. All the way into Nevada and then they keep on going from there. There's all kinds of things in places like that where people don't go. Most of them stay where they should stay. But New Harmony has its share of spirits and such."

"What kind of spirits?"

"There's been plenty through the years. So people say.

But I've only seen one. A creature black as night and covered in flames, but never eaten up by them. I saw it right out there in the woods you're poking around in."

"Nope, I haven't seen anything like that at all."

The rest of the meal was silent.

IV

The next morning, Jake went to the backyard, as was becoming his daily ritual. He circled the treehouse tree and walked the perimeter of the woods, becoming lost in thought.

"Hello," came a voice, making him jump.

He swung toward the woods to see a young girl, about his age he guessed, standing at the edge of the tree line. She looked at him, not appearing frightened of him in the least now. Her curly red hair fell just past her shoulders and framed a genuine, kind smile. Her skin was pale, and freckles dotted her cheeks.

"Hi," he said. He was not used to speaking to girls and felt himself flush.

"My name's Aideen."

"I'm Jake. . . . Um . . . do you live around here?"

"I used to live in a house over there, past the woods," she said, pointing north through the trees. "Now I'm just here for the summers mostly. It's too cold in the winter. I don't like the cold. But I like to wander through the woods in the summer. It's peaceful. I hope I didn't scare you."

"No. No. I was just thinking."

"About what?"

"Nothing really. I just like to come out here in the morning and think. There's not much to do around here."

"Yeah, that's why I like to walk. I have to go. I'll come back. I come by here a lot. I like you," she said.

Jake was startled, as much by her "I like you" as by her

abrupt departure.

"Okay, bye," he said quickly and watched her head into the trees.

He did hope to see her again.

V

Over the following week Jake frequently heard noises coming from downstairs at night; his uncle walking the rooms he guessed. He heard footsteps up and down the short hall, occasionally stopping for a time, a door opening or closing, and once he heard rattling that he could not identify. Often as he drifted to sleep, he heard the sound of a bird or a raccoon on the roof, scratching and scraping. His mind, he was sure, would play tricks on him in the early haze of sleep, bringing the noise much closer.

One morning at breakfast, he asked his uncle about his nighttime activity. His uncle gave him a questioning look.

"I'm not up at night," he said. "I'm asleep before you judging from your light, unless you've taken to sleeping with your light on."

VI

Aideen was true to her word. She returned frequently, often catching Jake in the morning for a quick hello or lingering with him for a longer talk. She told him about her family, the house they had owned and lived in nearby, her school. But mostly she talked about the woods, the walks she would take, the insects and animals and trees, the paths she would discover, the way the light changed through the trees as the day moved on. He was fascinated by her and hung on her words. He was hungry for a friend and, more so, delighted that Aideen would go out of her way to spend time with him.

VII

May wore quickly into June. The days were warmer, the crickets and frogs louder at night. By mid-June, Aideen and Jake had a near daily ritual of taking walks through the woods behind the house. Never too far, but always discovering something new. A stream, a large, old hollowed-out tree that one of them could comfortably fit inside, a new insect or animal. And there was always conversation. He loved this most. Back home, he could not get a girl to look at him, much less hold a real conversation. He was lonely there. But more than that, he felt weird. He felt ugly. He felt alien and disgusting to everyone but his very small circle of friends. But here he had Aideen. He stared at her as she knelt among the trees, looking at a colorful leaf or discarded snail shell. She was beautiful. Her flame red hair and pale skin were the most beautiful contrast he could imagine. He could not believe she was hanging out with him. He had to drive all the way through the state to the middle of nowhere to get a girl to speak to him, and that girl was beautiful.

Looking up at him at that moment she smiled. "Come sit with me." And of course, he did.

Sitting together in the dirt, smiling sweetly at him, she reached over and grabbed his hand. His heart raced. His eyes widened. He had never really been touched by a girl before. He had never been to a school dance. Never kissed. Never held hands. He had thought of these things so many times, hoped he could have them, but was sure that he would be the lonely weirdo the rest of his life. He sat looking at her hand encircling his. He was sure he was sweating.

"Do you want me to stop?" she asked, looking worried.

"No! No!" he stammered.

She smiled. "I like you. A lot. You're kind. You're interesting. You let me talk about all kinds of things and never look bored. And your hand is warm. I like how it feels."

"Uh, I like how yours feels too," he said. He loved how it felt, in fact. He wished he could sit here all night holding it.

They sat in the dirt among the trees, light dancing through the leaves in the warm summer air talking about nothing in particular, and Jake could not have been happier. Some time later, as the sun made its way to the west and the light began to change, turning gray and illuminating their surroundings considerably less, Aideen looked around and pulled her hand back from his. He felt disappointed and empty, but these feelings evaporated as she moved quickly forward and kissed him. Her lips touched his. He felt his face tingle and his cheeks flush with heat. She smiled at him with her sweet smile.

"It's getting late. It will be dark in a while. I can't be here after dark. I've got to go. I hope to see you again tomorrow. I like you, Jake. A lot."

And with that, she rose and began to walk away.

"I like you too," he called to her, not knowing what else to say.

He watched her walk back in the direction they had come, but he remained sitting, relishing the memory of her touch and her kiss. He sat there until the light was nearly gone, then picked himself up and walked home.

VIII

Night was falling on the house when he made his way back. The joy of the day washed away as dark lay claim on the surrounding woods.

He resisted sleep, trying to hang on to the day. But his tired mind succumbed, and his eyes began to droop before a noise jerked him awake and upright. He listened, heart racing.

A loud bang sounded from the first floor of the house. Then footsteps, hard and fast.

"Where are you?" his uncle's voice growled loudly from below.

He heard the door of the screened porch slam. Jake flew to the window and looked out. His uncle stood on the back lawn perfectly still, fists raised to his side. Then his uncle began pacing in a lengthening line back and forth on the lawn, looking around, out to the woods, to the treehouse, and back to the porch, his head swiveling as he walked.

Jake watched his uncle with growing fear until another sound caught his attention. Footsteps again downstairs.

Jake swung around toward the trapdoor opening that led to the first floor. He looked at the dark rectangular hole in the floor, but could not see down from his angle by the window. He heard it again. Footsteps, small and quick in the short hallway below him. Then the unmistakable creaking sound of someone putting weight on the folding stairs. Someone directly below him. Coming up.

His uncle screamed again from the back lawn. "Get out of here! Go!"

Another sound from the stairs. Another creak. Jake stood frozen, looking at the black opening on the floor. Another creak. Jake reached for something, anything, to defend himself. His grasping hand found a book on his desk and he held it up in front of him, not sure if it was a shield or a weapon.

He stood that way for what felt like several minutes. No more creaking, but no sound of retreat either from below. He could not hear his uncle now and could not look away from the opening on his floor to see where he was. He stood. Breathing. Staring at the black opening on the floor.

Then a sound of quick movement. Creak, creak, creak, ascending the stairs. Coming fast. Jake tightened his grip on the book.

He saw a figure. The sound of burning paper, insect wings, and dried leaves filled the room. Something black and shadowy lurched from the stairs and forward. Smokey and enveloped in ash, swirling and solid. It dashed toward him, seeming to fly through the air. He caught a glimpse of red before it hit him. Bare tissue, raw, bleeding. As it collided with him his breath caught and he could not inhale. He gagged and coughed. His eyes burned and he felt pressure on his chest, his stomach, his head, like the thing was trying to push into him or go straight through him.

He staggered back against the wall, dropping the book, flailing his arms in front of him, striking at the figure, choking to breathe. Sulfur, ash, and pain filled his lungs. He coughed and spit black onto the floor, and the specter was gone.

He slumped to the floor, retching and gagging. His eyes, stinging and watering, darted around the room. Nothing. But again, the putrid smell. Burning hair and rubber. Charred meat.

He looked out the window. His uncle was not there. He did not hear movement below. He darted to the stairs, lifting them, and closing the trapdoor.

He did not sleep that night.

IX

Early the next morning, as the sun began to softly illuminate his room, he opened the trapdoor, lowered the stairs, and crept down. He found his uncle asleep on the porch. Jake's sleep-deprived mind reeled with the events of the previous night. He could taste ash and decay.

Aideen did not come around in the morning as Jake had hoped she would. He waited for hours in the backyard, sitting at the foot of the tree under the treehouse. He needed her comfort today. He thought of the touch of her hand and the kiss. He loved these memories. But this was not what he wanted today. He wanted simply to see her, to talk to her. He wanted to be told that it would be okay. He was confused and frightened, and she was solace.

He dozed against the tree. Awakening, the sun had gone considerably further west. The light had begun its metamorphosis from the revealing yellow of the day to the paler tones of afternoon when Aideen finally emerged from the woods. He scrambled up and raced to her. His words came out like a torrent.

"Something happened last night. Something came into my room. My uncle was acting crazy. He was screaming at something. Running around the yard. I think he saw something. I think it may be the thing I saw in the treehouse when I first got here. I saw a thing up there. I saw a shape and smelled something burning. I smelled the same thing last night when the thing came to my room. It hit me. I think it's the burning monster my uncle talked about."

Jake was near panic trying to recount the events of last night and the past months. Aideen's face etched with worry. She asked questions, slowing him down and piecing together his experiences.

Then she paused, staring into his eyes for a full minute before speaking.

"There is no monster. I've walked around these woods for years. But there is a story," Aideen began with deliberate calm. "There's the old story about the girl who died . . . was killed. Some say she was killed by a homeless guy or by a crazy neighbor. Some think she was killed by someone she loved. Someone she trusted. They all say she was burned. She was burned alive, and she's still around here somewhere." Aideen paused. "They all say it feels really cold when you burn."

Jake stared at her, unsure what to say. She rose and began to walk away, but turned back, looking worried and upset.

"It's getting dark. I have to go."

She left Jake feeling alone and confused. She did not give him comfort as he had hoped. She gave him the story of a burned girl. Troubled and frightened, he went back to the house.

X

That evening he sat at his desk staring out the window. He was too distracted to read and too frightened to sleep. Downstairs was silent. No creaking floorboards or stairs. No pacing. No yelling. Jake sat numbly watching the gray dusk turn to dark.

Then something moved.

A figure emerged from the woods and made its way to the lonely tree. It mounted the ladder and moved briskly up into the treehouse.

Jake did not hesitate. He darted down his stairs, passed down the hall and into the yard. He did not know what he wanted to do, but he knew that he had to see what this was.

Although the sun had set and darkness owned the woods surrounding him, the treehouse was lit by a dull gray light.

Jake ascended the ladder.

He jutted his head through the trapdoor and gagged at the stench of sulfur and burnt things. Then the soft sound of rustling leaves. Paper. Insect wings and scuttling legs. The inside of the treehouse was illuminated by a soft red-yellow glow that flickered dimly around him. He saw someone hunched over in a corner, facing away.

Oh, God, he thought. Aideen.

She was hunched over, shaking, almost convulsing in unnatural movement, lacking structure, like nothing was holding her together. Her red, curled hair streamed behind her. Parts of her jutted out at odd angles as other parts sunk in. Her body flowed, undulating and spasming. She sank slowly to the floor and turned her head to look at him. Tears streamed down her face. His own tears mirrored hers. Then her face began to blacken.

    He stood on the ladder, staring and frozen in place watching her transform, the pale tone of her skin darkening. Cracks opened in her cheeks, her forehead, her neck. Her tears turned to steam, and her skin peeled away. Her eyes sank in. Her beautiful hair turned to soot and floated off. He was rooted in horror as her clothing followed her hair, revealing the blackened form of her body to match her face. She raised her hands, also blackened and cracked, as if shielding herself, and he saw cracked flesh fall from her, revealing deep red muscle beneath.

    Not her. No.

    He propelled himself up the remaining few rungs of the ladder into the treehouse. The mound in front of him was a kaleidoscope of raw and burnt flesh churning itself, no trace of Aideen remaining.

    He took a step forward.

    The churning stopped. The burnt flesh swirled around the red, raw lump, then rose like a column from the floor. The sound of crackling fire grew louder. The blackened exterior swelled, no longer a formless mass on the floor. The thing stood, wisps of smoke rising off the vaguely human form. Jake thought that it was looking at him, although there were no eyes or features to confirm this.

    He became aware that he was crying.

    The thing moved toward him.

    No, not a thing. Aideen.

    He remembered the night in his room. The terror as this thing lunged toward him. The feeling of it pressing into him. And his resistance. He fought. He was terrified and hated it.

    But he did not hate her.

    Aideen.

    He remembered the afternoon in the woods and the touch of her hand and her lips.

    Aideen moved closer.

Jake stepped back, fear tightening his stomach.

Aideen.

Tears ran down his face from the growing burn of sulfur. From fear, sadness, love.

"I love you," he said.

He fell to his knees as the thing, Aideen, moved closer. He opened his arms. He would not choke and cough this out of his lungs. He would not push it away. He knelt as it—she—approached and was upon him. The swirling black exterior pressed into him and gave way to the crust of broken, burnt flesh beneath. This, in turn, cracked revealing raw red and white streaked tissue. He breathed deeply, his lungs burning, eyes pouring tears. He wanted to gag at the burnt flesh, burnt hair, swirling smoke, and sulfurous sting, but he would not allow it. He breathed in.

Aideen pressed further, and crisp exterior flesh gave way to softness beneath. The softness moved into him. He felt her penetrate through his mouth, his nose, his eyes, his skin. He felt warm. She felt warm. She felt the scarring fires die and the burning cold soften to warmth. He was full and encased. They were warm. Jake shuddered violently and fell forward from his knees, prostrate on the floor and into darkness.

XI

They awoke in the morning on the floor of the treehouse, lying still and feeling the rough wood against their face. They felt the breeze through the window. They heard birds singing.

She used to tell us about the sounds of the birds in the woods, they thought.

Now they heard them together, hearing the song like they never had alone. They were no longer cold. They were no longer burning.

They stood up, made their way down the ladder, and went into the house.

They found the uncle seated at the kitchen table.

"How are you doing this morning?" the uncle asked, looking up briefly from coffee.

"We're fine. We're going to be just fine."

JUST DESSERTS

Katrina Hayes

A boy stands up and faces the group. He pushes his glasses higher on his nose. "My name is Harrison, and my sister passed away two months ago." He swallows and puts his hands in his pockets. "She wasn't very nice to me, and I'm feeling confused and guilty because I know I should miss her, but I . . . don't."

Harrison sits down. The group nods and mutters understanding.

The facilitator stands up, "Thank you for sharing, Harrison. Death is complicated for the living. All of us here . . ."

The facilitator goes on, but Harrison stops listening. He is seventeen, and he's thinking about Bernice, his elderly upstairs neighbor, who used to babysit him as a child and, as the years passed, became his closest friend. He's thinking about her and the journal she pushed into his hands the last time he saw her.

On that morning, Bernice knocked on their door to pick up his sister for a drive to an upstate university.

"Hide this," she had whispered.

His sister had come into the hall, purse on her shoulder, makeup done, and snarled at him as she closed the door in his face.

He had gone to his room and over the next hour turned page after page of Bernice's personal diary. Now, in the basement meeting room, there is one passage that keeps going through his mind.

In her neat cursive, Bernice had written, *I worry that if I don't intercede, his sister will kill him. I'm writing this to buoy myself to the cause of protecting him. I'm not being dramatic. If I need a reminder that the girl is a monster, all I have to do is go back through these pages. Or look at the scars on his body.*

    The meeting ends. Harrison gets up and shoves his hands into his pockets. Keeping his head down, he limps to the exit and up the stairs to the street. It's dark out and cold and people hurry, chins tucked into scarves and hats pulled down over ears. Harrison walks, deep in thought.

Before
"Harry?" Bernice says. "Let me see those."
Harrison holds his arms out where deep, angry scratches stand out red against his pale skin. They hurt.
"My God," Bernice says, and her face blanches. As she wipes the wounds with a warm, wet cloth, her lips press together until her mouth is nothing but a white line. "She did this to you?" Bernice asks, keeping her eyes on the scratches.
Harrison shrugs and Bernice looks him in the eye.
"Tell me the truth, Harry. Your sister did this, didn't she?"
Harrison nods. He is ten, and he is confused by how his big sister's rage comes over her and all she wants to do is hurt him.
"Did you tell your mother?" She asks.
Harrison shakes his head and talks fast and low. "She's more mean when I tell. She pinches me when they aren't looking, and once, I told mother when she pulled my hair, and then she came into my room that night and put a pillow over my face. She's scary."
Bernice's face turns a warm shade of red. "Well, We'll have to do something about that, won't we?"
At the end of his visit, he hugs her tight. "You're my best friend. You're the only one who understands."
Bernice hugs him back. "I'm always here for you, my boy."

Harrison comes to the door of his building and inserts his key. He takes the stairs, even though his leg throbs, for he is not able to stand still to wait for the elevator. Thoughts of his dead sister plague his memory, making it impossible for him to be still in this building full of dark souvenirs.

He climbs up the stairs toward the fifth floor, shuddering for only a moment when he passes the place where she pushed him when he was thirteen, breaking his leg and leaving him with a permanent limp.

Before
"Don't say anything, don't make her mad," Harrison says.

Bernice inhales through her nose and says, "She'll get what's coming to her," as she places a plate of tiny sandwiches in front of the young boy that she loves as her own child.

The cruelty has escalated. This time Harrison is twelve and has a broken finger. She hit it with a hammer. He had cried out in pain and she grabbed his forearm.

"You say one word," his sister had threatened.

Harrison had gasped on his sobs and nodded. When their father came to see what was wrong, Harrison said he had done it himself by accident. As he was taken out the door to the emergency room, his sister had smiled at him.

Harrison unlocks the door to the apartment where he still lives with his mom and dad. He smells a pine tree and spice candle. He hears the sound of his dad's record player whirring and whirring at the end of a vintage vinyl and nothing else.

In the living room, his dad is asleep on the couch with a crocheted blanket over his lap. The kitchen is empty. He blows out the candle that has been left burning then goes into the bathroom and locks the door. He leans on the sink and looks into the mirror.

Before
"Oh, Harry," Bernice sits in the chair next to his hospital bed.

It is visiting hours, and his parents have gone home to rest.

Harrison winces as he adjusts himself. The scissors had missed his organs, going in just below his ribs on the left side. He was lucky that she didn't know what she was doing.

He is sixteen, and things were just starting to go okay for him at school. His aspirations to play baseball having been taken from him because of his leg injury, he had just joined the robotics club where he was surprised and pleased to find that he was rather gifted at the craft.

And now this.

"I hate her. I wish she were dead," Harrison whispers.

"I wish that too," Bernice says, and her eyes are fiery in the hospital lights.

Harrison uses the bathroom and then peeks into his parent's room where the shape of his mother is buried under the blankets, snoring softly.

In his room, Harrison takes the journal that belonged to Bernice and reads the last entry for the thousandth time.

She has hurt you for the last time, Harry. I want you to know how much I love you. You're the most brilliant boy. You're kind and clever, and I'm sorry I failed to protect you from her. As a last gift, I give you the gift of freedom. Do amazing things, my boy. Be happy and live a good life. I love you.

Harrison lifts the newspaper article from where he has stashed it in the pages of the journal. On the front is a photo of a car buried under the front of a semi-truck. Two Dead in Head-On Collision the headline reads.

Bernice had volunteered to drive his sister for a University tour since his mom and dad were busy with work. Bernice had never intended to make it to the appointment, sacrificing herself while taking the life of his sister. That was her gift to him.

Harrison puts the article back inside the pages of the journal and places the book in its hiding place. He kicks off his shoes, places his glasses on the side table, and lies on his bed. He pulls the blankets over himself and smiles, free to rest at last.

"I love you too, Bernice."

MAN'S BEST FRIEND

Lori Shields

"You ever eat dog?"

"No."

"Well you should sometime. It makes you realize that you could eat your best friend if you had to. It's a freeing experience, really. Makes a man feel secure in this world of dwindling resources."

John steadied himself against the bar stool. A sudden wave of nausea made him queasy. But then what kind of person did he expect could be hired for this sort of job?

"I want you to be kind," John whispered. "Don't let her see it coming."

The man narrowed his eyes.

"You want it done a certain way, you should have said sooner. I got my methods. You want it done all beautiful and dignified, you should have hired a fucking interior decorator." He took a swig of John's beer, wiped his dripping mouth on his sleeve, and laughed, "She never would have seen that coming."

John's heart sank.

"At the very least, make it quick."

John felt trapped in a loveless marriage. He remembered sitting at the table on their anniversary watching her chew forty times on a piece of meat. He counted. She always chewed exactly forty times. Good for the digestion, she claimed.

That's when he thought, twenty-five years. Twenty-five fucking years. How had he gotten here? What was he doing here with her anyway? He remembered telling her he'd be glad to go to the prom with her since her regular beau was off with the Navy. And the next thing he knew, twenty fucking five years had passed. Twenty-five years of methodical chewing. And precision bed making, spotless floors, perfectly draped curtains, flawlessly prepared meals, and crisply pressed shirts. His home looked like an up-scale hotel room—devoid of warmth or character. And the monthly lovemaking left him feeling guilty, like he owed her something for the big favor she'd just done for him.

Their white miniature poodle, Mandy, was the only authentic thing in the house.

When Sabrina had first brought Mandy home, John thought she was a frivolous expenditure, but one day, while he watched Mandy wipe her butt along the carpeting, it dawned on him how much he loved that dog. She might jump up on the coffee table to snatch a bite of cake, and so what if she shredded a few socks? He realized he loved her. She was uncouth, willful, and disgusting, and John admired her for it. She was the true light of his life.

John knew that Mandy was fond of him as well. He was sure of it. She came when he called, completely ignoring Sabrina's whinny whistle. She was attentive to his moods, always laying her head on his thigh while he recovered from a flu or rotten day at work. Sure, secreting pieces of his dinner under the table past Sabrina's watchful eye probably had worked its charm, but still, he felt Mandy loved him despite his little indulgences.

"That will be ten thousand now and another ten after I complete the job."

John slid a thick envelope along the bar.

"Fine," said the man. "You be gone by noon, Saturday. I'll be off the premises by 2. Now if you grow pussy feet, call me before 10 a.m. that morning. I keep this dough whether you call it off or not. You know how to reach me."

John stared at his drink. He couldn't bring himself to look into the eyes of the last man his wife would ever see.

"Yeah. I know."

The next four days, John tried to act normal. The perfunctory morning kiss on the cheek, the wave goodbye from the window as he left for work, the traditional toy tussle with Mandy in the doorway when he got home, the perfunctory greeting kiss, the dinner with the chewing, a numbing glass of brandy with a magazine in the evening. The perfunctory good night kiss. All in order. Nothing amiss.

But as Saturday grew closer, John's guilt grew.

Friday evening, trying to regain the justification, John forced himself to watch his wife eat. He wanted to count the number of times she chewed to remind himself of all the ways he hated her. But as he watched, he couldn't help but feel sorry for her. He knew she would be dead in a little less than twenty-four hours. He watched as this delicately-boned creature sitting on death row innocently opened her mouth like a baby bird to accept a fork full of meat. She started chewing.

John forced himself to count, one, two, three, four . . . Then she suddenly stopped, cocking her head to one side. An embarrassed smile creased the corners of her mouth. She started to reach for her water glass but then thought the better of it. She looked at him, her eyes growing large as her smile disappeared. She reached for her throat with one hand, then two.

John shook from his trance. He jumped up and ran to her side of the table. Her eyes, twisted in terror, were glued to his the entire time. He grabbed her shoulders and pulled her from her chair, turned her backside to him and wrapped his arms around her.

How the hell is this done? he thought.

He made a fist with one hand and wrapped the other hand around it, then pushed them into his wife's slender body. He feared he might crack her ribs, but he figured it was worth the chance. Nothing happened and Sabrina was losing consciousness. He could feel her slump against him. Figuring he had nothing to lose, he jerked her even harder, pushing upwards as he squeezed. The sudden thrust sent the piece of meat flying across the carpeting. He gently lowered Sabrina to the floor as Mandy darted across the room and swallowed the murderous morsel in one gulp.

Sabrina lay silently for only a moment, then violently gasped, coughing as she exhaled. Only then did John realize how very terrified he had been. Kneeling next to Sabrina, he took her in his arms.

She clung to him.

"Oh, John," she croaked. "John, I've been so stupid."

She swallowed again. "All these years I've been waiting."

"Waiting? What are you talking about?"

"I thought you knew that I had lied to you, and that is why you didn't love me. And I've been trying to make it up to you. I've been trying to make your life perfect in hopes that one day you would fall in love with me."

"What lie, Darling?" Trying to calm her, he stroked her hair.

"I never had a beau in the Navy. It was just an excuse to get you to take me to the prom. I knew you never really loved me, but I have loved you since the minute I met you in chemistry class. You have always been so kind and thoughtful. But I lied to you. I tricked you into marrying me. I knew you didn't love me. I am such a terrible person. . . . but just now . . . what you did . . . you could have let me die, but you didn't. You truly love me."

She grabbed him behind the neck and kissed him with such passion that he had to pull away from her to double-check that he was with his wife.

That night, for the first time in their marriage, they made passion-filled love.

In the morning, while they cuddled on the couch next to Mandy, John texted the man to call off the job. Minutes later the doorbell rang. John threw on his robe and answered the door. It was the man.

"What are you doing here?"

"I could ask you the same thing. You were supposed to be gone by now, bowling or something."

"It's six in the morning. Nobody bowls at six a.m. Besides," John leaned into the man and whispered, "I called off the hit."

The man backed up and raised his voice. "Look, dude, I came all the way out here to your fancy neighborhood to get this job done. I want to be compensated for my time and energy. That seems fair, don't it?"

"Fine. How much do you think your 'time and energy' are worth?"

Sabrina had walked up behind her husband and wrapped her arms around his waist. "Who's your friend?" she asked.

"Just a business contact, Hon." John gave her a gentle squeeze. "He and I have some business to attend to in the study. Can you give us a few minutes?"

"Sure," she said, pulling away from him.

John and the man walked to the study and closed the door.

"How much do you need to go away?"

"I figure the balance is due. It's the traveling that takes my time. The rest of the job is quick and easy. Enjoyable, really."

"Fine," said John.

He fumbled around in the top drawer of his desk until he found a key. Turning his back to the man, he unlocked a filing cabinet and rifled through a drawer. It was filled with passports, credit cards, and a large pile of cash, larger than ten thousand. Much larger.

"Ten thousand, right?"

Later that evening, the man was sitting at John's table finishing a meal he had made for himself. Mandy cocked her head to one side to look at him with curiosity.

The man asked, "You ever eat human?"

He tossed her a piece of his dinner. She swallowed the murderous meat in one gulp.

MORNING MEDITATION

Scott Bryan

I talked with her.

The highlight of last year was the League of Utah Writer's Quill conference. I never have the time to do squat, and the one time I actually broke my boring schedule, guess what happened?

She happened.

Kara Gordon. Long, luscious brown hair like a chocolate waterfall, an open smile that lit my heart like the sun breaking through heavy, dark clouds, and those eyes! The minute I locked onto those peepers, my soul became trapped deep within a world of excitement and contagious happiness.

I'd never met a soul quite like her, before or after.

It's not like I ever get many chances to meet someone like her. I work nights emptying trucks and stocking shelves at my local grocery store. boring but it the monotony gives me a chance to plan out the Sci Fi novel that's just burning to get out.

When one of the guys at work mentioned a local writer's conference, I took a chance. Maybe I'd get through this manuscript. Maybe I'd finally just sit down and finish this damn thing.

Well, I did learn a bunch of stuff. Felt inspired, gained new ideas on how to break through the blockage and keep going. I even met some fellow writers and felt pretty fired up.

But all of that paled compared to what happened on my last day. The very first class I took was Morning Meditation and Writer Wellbeing. It was taught by one of my favorite authors,

Johnny Worthen. I was looking forward to meeting him and asking him to sign my copy of his book, but all my plans vanished.

See, when I sat down, at first, I became enthralled in the class. As the jovial tie-dyed scribe energetically enthused about various ways to be at one with my inner being, my outer being couldn't stop stealing glances at the girl sitting next to me.

Kara smiled and laughed, and each and every time she did, I felt pulled into her spiritual gravity. I suppose I was lucky. She seemed so engrossed in the lecture that she didn't notice the goof staring at her like some maladjusted pervert.

Then Johnny wanted us to calm ourselves, breathe in and out and let everything go. I sure wonder what would've happened if she wasn't in that class. Would I have mastered total control of my thoughts? Learned to focus inward, push away self-doubt and become my own Zen Writing Master?

Who knows?

I was lost at the very beginning of class. As I sat there with my eyes closed, instead of focusing on my breathing, or calming my body, or even a personal happy place, all I could see in my head was her. Instead of letting go of my thoughts or fears, I built them up. I kept going over and over in my head how I could start a conversation with her.

After the lecture ended, everyone began to shuffle into the open foyer. I had my chance! After all that practice in my head, I still felt like an awkward fool, but I couldn't let her disappear.

I stumbled out, "I'm Steve how are you that was a fun class what's your name?"

Yeah. I want to be an author, and I can't even speak with punctuation.

Once again, her laugh pulled me in. She replied, "I'm Kara Gordon. You're funny. I need to get to another class in Summit. Want to walk with me?"

"Yes!" my extra loud reply betrayed my total lack of cool. I tried to correct my failing image. "I mean, I could walk. Summit. That's the one past the bar, right?"

She smiled. "Yes. I love this conference. I attend every year without fail. So where are you from?"

We navigated around various attendees as we approached the open staircase. "I'm from Sugarhouse. You?"

Instead of answering, she asked, "What brings you to the Quills conference, Steve from Sugarhouse?"

Her question threw me, but of course I was ready for a clever, thought-out answer, "Um . . . writing?"

She laughed. "I figured that, silly. But what kind of writing? What do you hope to learn?"

"Well, everything. I have about four thousand words down on the next Sci Fi classic if I could just learn where to go with it." We continued through the bar and down the hallway towards Summit. "I'm stuck in the middle; I think I'm not showing enough, and I can't seem to buckle down and finish it."

"You certainly have a lot of work to do." She smiled as we stopped at the open door to Summit. "But you'll get it. Well, the class just started, so I'll meet you after, ok?"

As "Mr. Seize the Opportunity" I nodded and watched her enter. I began to walk down the hall, still stunned when my incredible stupidity struck me. I spun on my heels, went back to join her, and stopped at the front of the class.

Awkwardly, the speaker stopped in mid-sentence. I felt the entire room's eyes on me. Why was it so hot suddenly? The staff at the Marriott really needed to get the air conditioning fixed.

I pushed down my embarrassment to quickly scan the class for her, but to my disappointment she was nowhere to be found. I awkwardly found a seat in the back but couldn't focus on the presentation on work/life balance by author Jared Quan. Nothing the speaker said stuck in my head. All I could think about was her.

The rest of the conference, I searched and searched, but I never found her. For a year I marched through the monotony, but this time a glimmer of hope twinkled in the back of my mind.

Her words reverberated in my thoughts. "I attend every year

without fail."

Twelve months. Eleven. Ten. Each one passed by, and I was closer to my second chance.

After 365 eternal days, I was back at the Marriott University Park hotel. Once again, I was at the Quills Conference, and once again, I searched for Kara. I asked so many people, but no one had heard of her.

Finally, I found myself dejected, sitting in a chair in the conference atrium. A friendly voice spoke up, "Hey, are you alright?"

I looked up to see a man with a name badge that read Daniel Yocom. I replied, "I'm looking everywhere for a girl named Kara Gordon. She says she always comes to the conference, but her name's not on the app, and I can't find her anywhere."

The color drained from Daniel's face as he replied, "I'm sorry. I knew her. I'm afraid she died five years ago."

Did I imagine last year? I couldn't have. It was real. She was real. Wasn't she?

TO NEW LIVES

Daniel Yocom

"Do you feel that, Jeff?" Deb's hand waved side to side in front of his face.

"The house is old, and the boards on the porch are a little loose. That's not a problem." Jeff rocked back on his heels making the boards squeak.

"Jeff." Deb stepped back from the open front door.

"If it becomes a problem for you, I can ask the agency to see if I can hammer in some nails to get rid of the noise." He continued to rock on the planking.

"Jeffery?" Deb turned away from the door to face Jeff with her hands resting on her rounding belly.

"Not the porch." Jeff scanned the area of their temporary home the adult foster placement agency helped them with. "Deb?"

"You don't feel anything strange about the aura of this place?" Deb cocked her head. She already knew what her husband's answer would be.

"No. What do you feel?" Jeff set down the suitcase he was carrying.

Deb knew Jeff was all about the computer programming and logic problems. He was good at them. He probably still didn't believe how she could sense people and energies. At least he listened now without making fun of her.

"Something here doesn't want us to go in. It's pushing on me to keep me out, to keep us out." She pressed her hand against the energy she felt emanating from the doorway.

"Okay." Jeff turned towards the door and stretched out his hand. "I don't feel anything. I'm not saying you don't. Just I don't. I'll go first, and we'll see what happens."

Jeff picked up the suitcase and took a step towards the open door. He stood at the threshold and leaned into the house. Deb had no idea what he would be looking for. Deb moved her hand along the wall. She knew she could push through the energy. Jeff was standing in it.

The pressure under Deb's hand released, like a beach ball deflating, as Jeff stepped into the house. The force was still there, but weaker. Deb could sense something or someone had reluctantly given up on keeping them out of the house.

She followed Jeff through the barren entryway and into the living room. A couple of small throw rugs had been added, but the rest of the furniture looked, and felt, like it was the original furnishing. The furniture had been moved from where it must have been sitting for years. Deb could see the traffic pattern worn on the hardwood floor.

Jeff spun slowly around and smiled. "It looks good in here. I'll check out the rest of the house." Deb smiled and nodded.

Using the floor as her guide, Deb slid the furniture around until it fit the pattern while she waited for Jeff to come back.

"You shouldn't be moving heaving stuff around. But, hey, this looks a lot better this way. Maybe you should consider studying interior design when our grants come through for school next year. You can look over the rest of the rooms and see what you would like to do with them, but please let me move the stuff around for you. I don't want you to hurt yourself and, well, you know." Jeff gently rested his hand on Deb's shoulder.

"I'm fine. None of this was hard to move on the wood floors." To prove her point she gave the chair a push with her hand. Jeff's hand twitched on her shoulder. "But I promise I won't move anything on my own."

"Thanks. This place looks like it could be a thrift store. There is a lot of old stuff here, like the furniture, but nothing that looked in really good shape. Except the mattress, it looks like its brand new. Let's look around so you can see where you want to put our stuff when I bring it in."

"Sounds good."

Deb looked around the room and sensed the furniture was where it should be. She could see where pictures had been hanging on the wall and been removed by the pattern left on the old wallpaper.

Deb stepped up on the porch and could feel the pressure emanating from the house had lessened even more. It had been a long morning of taking Jeff to work and then to her checkup. She hoped she could rest better than the night before. It wasn't the first time in her life she had dreams of being alone. She was sure many orphans had those types of dreams. Talking about dreams and the fears of being alone was how she connected with Jeff years ago when they were in junior highschool. She hadn't had such a vivid dream since finishing highschool.

She clicked on the coffeemaker to heat up the remains from earlier. The kitchen was always considered the heart of the home—the hearth. This one was no exception. It was intimate, with a two person round wooden table. It was as though it never expected to have more than two people in it.

With her mug in hand, Deb made her way back into the living room. She was going to sit in the smaller overstuffed chair and suddenly changed her mind to sit on the couch under the front window.

The afternoon light lit up the room. She looked at the placement of the furniture. She placed her mug on a coaster on the coffee table in front of her and examined how the overstuffed and wingback chairs sat opposite her. Those chairs had been used a lot according to the wear on the floor. There was something about them and where they sat that gave Deb comfort. She picked her coffee up and leaned back into a pillow.

The wallpaper was an art deco pattern like the one on that skyscraper in New York. Deb thought it was probably something from the depression era. It was something to think the wallpaper was getting close to a hundred years old. It had seen a lot. Deb took a closer look at the faded patterns and nail holes of what had hung on the wall. There were different levels of fading as items were added and removed over time.

Three ovals drew her attention. All three were between the two chairs, sitting above the small table there. A larger one in the middle that was wider than taller, and a smaller one on each side that was narrower in width and slightly taller than the one in the middle. They had been placed as a set.

The kitchen may be the heart of the house, Deb felt this room to be where the soul of the house had been kept.

The coffee seemed to evaporate into the ether. Instead of getting another cup, Deb emptied the remains of the pot down the drain and turned her attention to exploring the house they would be in for probably the next year. She wanted to get the place straightened out like the front of the house.

Most of the house looked and felt right. There were a few pieces out of place, like someone had moved them to clean and didn't move them back. Deb would have Jeff straighten them up after she picked him up from work. He would feel good about doing it for her.

Deb wanted to explore the basement and the attic, but they would have to wait until tomorrow.

The basement stored the furnace, odds and ends, and a lot of empty mason jars. One of Deb's foster parents bottled fruit from an apricot tree when she was younger. She didn't care for the apricots, but there was a sense of being in a home and part of a family while helping them clean and stuff the jars with fruit. Growing reminiscent, Deb grabbed another cup of coffee and went into the back yard.

There stood two old trees, an apple and a peach. Withering blossoms dotted the branches of the peach while the apple was covered with blooms. The aroma drew Deb back to her earlier life being shuffled from one foster house to another.

Deb mentally shook herself. There was no way she was going to give in to those feelings again. Life was rough enough without entertaining despair and the idea she would be alone her entire life. What she could do is create new memories and experiences. If the agency would allow it, she was going to use the jars in the basement to bottle up the fruit. That is what Mrs. Cotrell did for her family with the apricots.

Goosebumps ran up Deb's arms as the spring breeze turned chilly. Deb went to get a sweater even though it looked like it was going to be a beautiful sunny day.

Jeff's sweatshirt was comfortable, warm, and provided a strange sense of security as Deb stood with her hand on the handle of the door that led up to the attic. Other memories poured in of the ghost stories Donald, another family's son, like to tell. There was always a ghost or a crazy person in the attic. What was worse, Deb could feel the presence of something, again, pushing back on her.

Today was different. There was a second energy pulling her in.

She hadn't seen a light switch and retrieved a flashlight. Shining the beam up the stairs, Deb grabbed the rail with her free hand and cautiously lifted her foot onto the first step. Feelings swept over and through her—a mix of fear and relief. Deb couldn't tell for sure if they were her feelings or were pressed upon her. Now she needed to see what was stored under this roof.

A bare bulb hung on wires from the rafters. Deb pulled the cord that seemed to float down from the fixture. The string snapped from her fingers as light filled the space and created dancing shadows as the light swung back and forth. Boxes and loose items were divided into three piles in the larger open space of the attic.

Deb checked out the first pile which had a cardboard sign with "dump" written on it with a large black marker. Dust covered everything in and out of the boxes. It probably was pulled out of the corners of the attic and just piled together. Most were broken things, probably planned to be repaired and subsequently forgotten about. Deb sighed.

A box written with "shop" sat under several others. She unfolded the flaps of the top one to see what it held. It was filled with clothes. With a quick restacking of the boxes, she was able to check the rest. There were mostly clothes and small knickknacks. Clearly items that could be sold through a thrift or consignment shop.

Pushed against the railing next to the steps was a box with a "?" written on it. Inside were framed pictures. Deb carefully pulled out a larger oval frame. A black and white wedding picture. A young couple, probably around the same age as her and Jeff, stood in front of a wooden arch with a flowering vine.

She pulled out two matching oval frames. They contained individual pictures of the couple. They were older. Deb could feel the love the couple had for each other from the pictures she was looking at. The rest of the frames were pictures of different places with the couple in different times of their life. She lined them up from when they were younger to their older years. They always smiled and held each other. There was joy, peace, contentment radiating from them. That is the life Deb wanted to have with Jeff.

Deb realized there were no pictures of children. Her sight went blurry as she placed her hand on her stomach and the child within. She used her sleeve to clear the tears from her eyes as she carefully placed all but the first three pictures back in the box.

"I found some pictures of a couple who I think used to live here." Deb timed her statement until Jeff had a mouthful.

"I guess that's good. I would think they would have cleared all that sort of stuff out before allowing anyone to use this place." He took another bite of potatoes.

"I called the agency about it before coming to pick you up tonight. The lady couldn't tell me much. All she knew was someone bought the house from the state and had given them a great lease to allow young couples in need help to get started."

"Don't you mean the estate, not state?"

"I asked the same thing. They said it they were pretty sure it was from the state, and it might have been some lawyer who bought it to use as a tax write off."

"Well, we lucked out then. A job, medical, school, and a place to live all wrapped up in one place. You've got that far away look. What else is there?"

"Nothing. Yet. I'm going to do some research if I can find out some more. I think this is all part of the energy I was feeling when we arrived. I'm also going to look up stuff on bottling peaches and making jam. The tree out back looks like it will be loaded. And when I was getting the mail from the box, the neighbor, Sally, greeted me. They've been here only a couple of years, and we are the first people here. Oh, she said she would help me with the peaches."

"Remember, this place is only temporary." Jeffs dropped his look away from Deb.

"I know the house is only temporary. And friendships might only last while we are here. Then again, we maintained a friendship through how many foster homes?"

"Point taken. I forgot to tell you earlier—one of the guys I work with is going to give me a ride so it will free you up. That should help as you dig into the history of the people who lived here. You really think it relates to the energy force field you felt?"

"The energy force field has changed its frequency as I explored the quadrants of the domicile and discovered strange new things. At one point the repulsion beam was also a tractor beam."

Jeff stopped chewing and cocked his head to the side. "Have you been reading my sci-fi books?"

Deb smiled broadly.

"I'm so happy you are home. Just a few minutes until dinner. It's another recipe from Sally. I also found some articles and the obituaries of the Harold and Maude Alabaster. They're on the table if you want to read them."

"They were quite community minded. Looks like they gave everything away but this place. And no kids to pass it on to."

"And that becomes a dark hole for finding out more. Ownership of this place is tied up in the courts, and the librarian couldn't find anything except it is in some type of holding where it can't be sold, but it can be used by a state-sponsored nonprofit. Which is why we have the chance to live here."

"There seems to be a number of strange coincidences of how we ended up here. Maybe your energy friends are helping us out."

"I've had an idea. Hear me out. I know it is going to sound kooky to you."

Jeff nodded and sat down.

"The Alabasters didn't have any family beyond themselves. We don't have any family beyond ourselves. Neither of us ever got adopted. But we can adopt them now. I know it sounds silly, but I feel like they could have been grandparents of one of us. I asked the agency about the pictures, and they didn't know what to do with them. We can have them if we want."

Deb checked the pots on the stove. There was a warmth in the kitchen. Fresh spring evening air caused the curtains to flutter. Deb felt like this was a home, the first real home feeling she had ever had. She finally turned towards her husband and saw him wipe a tear away.

"Yes, that sounds good. No, that feels good."

THE LAST GOODNIGHT

Steve Prentice

The Last Goodnight
the finality
 of the soft whisper, goodnight,
hangs in my mind the
night you closed your eyes one last
time haunts my dreams and paints my
days a hazy gray.
So many words left unsaid, none
I regret more than
I love you.

TODAY, TOMORROW, AND THE NEXT

J.E. Zarnofsky

Renata ducked behind the wide willow trunk, clutching her crossbow to her chest. Every piece of experience buried beneath decades of domesticity told her she had been spotted. The heatwave from the explosion of fire against the back side of the trunk confirmed just that.

She tsked and swept a singed piece of hair behind her ear. Reaching a hand into her pouch, she pulled out a glowing green orb and twirled it between her fingers. The liquid bubbled and swirled inside the thin glass.

So much for a quiet final job.

When Renata had agreed to one last mission, after having enjoyed fifteen years of retirement from the path, she knew there would be complications. They wouldn't have asked for her help otherwise.

Upon receiving the offer, she was surprised that the Praesidium had found her after all those years, and more surprised that they swallowed their pride to ask her. Renata didn't recognize the messenger that came directly to their homestead and handed her the letter. She was relieved Aveline had planned to spend the day running errands in town.

Drawing her wife into the world she had left behind, all those years ago, was the last thing she wanted. She just had to make it home to her one last time. Then the shadowed weight of her past would vanish for good.

Renata's trance shattered, leaving her in the heat of the fight as the ground beneath her shook. Two mid-distance spells in a row, she mused. Whoever hunted her was unwilling to give up their own position. But at this range, it gave her a narrow area of where the target could possibly have been.

As she secured her crossbow in the crook of her hip and drew back the string, affixing it to the latch, she wondered to herself if anyone ever truly retired from the field. She'd only been given the basics for the job, leaving Renata without the information on the target that she usually preferred. Her handler hand only given her this: that the target frequented the abandoned mill in this area, and that they were an asset of the Order that had fallen off the map until now. Somehow the Praesidium had tracked them down after years of searching.

But Renata was never told why they needed her.

With a hint of amusement at the familiar pulse of battle, she slid the bolt into the bow and pressed the corked vial the tip in one practiced motion. Without missing a beat, she turned, knelt, and aimed high for the trees across the clearing. She pulled the trigger. The bolt loosed. Renata spun back to her cover.

And then, she ran.

The shatter of glass pierced the air. The hissing gas spread. The clearing surrounded by thick ancient trees shuddered from the poison leeching into it. The fire and acid would leave a scar on the perfectly framed battlefield for generations—a true shame.

Renata heard a yelp and a curse from her opponent. A yelp and a curse that froze her to the core, though she kept running. She immediately knew why it had to be her.

A single crossbow bolt pierced the king's heart, and Renata fled from the throne room up the winding stairs. Usually, she'd have had a better escape route planned. Usually she would have had a way to repel from the tower. Usually she wouldn't have been caught.

This job was in no way usual.

Not once did she look behind her. It didn't matter how many of the King's guards or how many members of the Order followed her. She reached an unlocked door and burst through, finding only one small window overlooking the loch. The storm-churned lake roared below.

Her death was certain in the hands of the guards moments behind her, as was the mission's failure. Having just assassinated the king of Haven, Augustus, her remaining purpose was clear: she needed to make certain that she was not captured. Alive or dead, if she were caught the line could eventually be traced back to the Praesidium and a century of their work would be for naught.

She believed in the cause. She believed in the world that they fought for. So without looking behind her as the rushing footsteps neared, she jumped. All she heard before the rush of water raged in her ears was a curse and scream of frustration.

Renata had always wondered how that job hadn't come back to haunt her. Though she never saw the face of the king's bodyguard, the voice crying out as she fell haunted her for a lifetime. Pieces fell into place. The target had disappeared to avoid punishment for their failure that day. And somehow it seemed that Renata had failed that day too. Despite ceasing her work, despite laying down her daggers and bows, and making certain no sign of her kills would ever be seen again, the Praesidium had been implicated.

It wasn't enough.

She rushed through the forest, leaping over fallen trees and sliding down the steep hills. It wasn't until her lungs burned beyond her ability to drown out the pain that she stopped running from the past. Her body pressed against the ground, beneath the scrub oak, and she formulated a plan.

Renata's heart pounded against her chest. Her skills had gone soft as she enjoyed her time as a wife. Everything long committed to muscle memory now required focused thought.

She could no longer plan while moving nor think three steps ahead while fighting. She needed this time to make a plan and survive.

Renata scanned the area, searching for something though she couldn't quite place her finger on what it was. Something defensible.

All that mattered was surviving today, tomorrow, and the next… returning to Aveline. And then she spotted it. A small cliff from where she could set up her ambush and force an advantage.

One week after Renata had killed King Augustus, she entered a bustling town nestled in the valley between two great mountains harboring a vast lake. Despite the serene landscape, she found no pleasure or relaxation from its sights. Every movement from the corner of her eye, every loud noise, every lingering glance left her ready to grab her dagger. Ready to add yet another body to the ever-growing count.

After she'd jumped, she floated down river through the storms for three and a half days and then hid in the hills for the same before arriving in Glenville. Long enough for her to be dead and for her pursuers to have given up the chase.

After stealing a chemise and burning her bloodied clothes, her sole possessions from her old life were her daggers strapped securely to her thighs. In the town, Renata spent time begging for a few coins and offering to do work for minimal pay. At first, she'd planned only to do enough to purchase some warmer traveling clothes and continue on her way east to Riven. Far from the clutches of the Praesidium and the Order. Far from where anyone would ever hear of King Augustus or his murder.

But then she met Aveline.

The first day they didn't exchange any words, but she felt the way that the quiet woman's gaze lingered on her. Renata pushed it off as nothing more than paranoia. On the second day, the woman with flaxen hair knelt before Renata and pressed three silver coins into her palm. Her fingers lingered as her rosy lips trembled a shy smile.

"What's your name?" the woman had asked.

Without a second thought Renata had answered and the woman stood up and walked away.

Regret immediately washed over Renata as she had given her identity, the only thing that was ever truly her own to this complete stranger. Her stomach clenched. Now she could be found. One of their death's had been sealed.

Renata followed the woman from a distance, keeping out of sight until the stranger stood at the door to the inn, fiddling with a worn skeleton key. After a moment, the key clicked and the woman vanished inside. A light flickered in a window as a lamp was lit. Renata stared at the window, her hands twitching as they hovered over the hilts of her daggers. Her cheeks flushed.

If she could stomach one more death, she'd be free.

That night, Renata packed the belongings she'd gathered into a small, stolen rucksack. It wasn't enough to get as far east as she wanted, but it could get her halfway there. She slung everything she owned onto her back and wrapped a woven wool blanket around her, clasping it at her neck with a roughly shaped penannular, and ducked back into the streets.

"Are you going travelin', at this time of night?" It was the woman from before. The one with her name.

Renata spun around and lunged at the woman. "Why are you following me?" The two slammed into the stone wall, and she pressed her forearm against the woman's throat. Her left hand freed a dagger from its sheath.

"I thought it was a cold night. That you might want somewhere warm to stay," she said through choked gasps.

Renata pressed harder, her arm on the oh-so-delicate throat of the terrified woman. "Who sent you?"

"None. I dunna know who you mean. I can leave, I . . ." The woman's forest green eyes rolled up into her head and her body collapsed into the cold mud. Renata took a step back. She studied the unconscious body. She could end it now. And then the horror washed over her. She dropped the dagger in her and gazed upon just what she had become.

An innocent woman who wanted nothing more than to help lay unconscious because of her fear, her anger, her blind faith that she could kill her way out of any situation.

She knelt in the mud and sheathed her dagger before fishing the skeleton key from the woman's pouch. Then she hoisted the woman over her shoulder, and headed to the inn.

Renata's only regret, as she crouched in wait, ready for her ambush, was that she had never told Aveline the truth. If she were to die there, in this fight fifteen years overdue, she'd never have the chance.

All the more reason to survive.

A concussive explosion set the stage as the first of her traps went off. One wouldn't be enough to stop her pursuer, that she knew, but the field would give her the advantage she needed in the fight.

She watched from her perch, noting the way the trees and brush jostled from her pursuers advance. With a deep breath she leapt from the cliff, drew her two long daggers, and thrust them deep into flesh.

The pig squealed. The animal panicked beneath her, bucking her off, both blades buried into its back. She landed on a rock, sharp pain shooting down her leg. The beast ran, taking her weapons, her safety, her only link to her old life, with it. Renata flattened herself to the ground, the tall grasses shielding her from view. She narrowed her eyes, scanning the area for her opponent. Or an escape.

An escape would be the one thing that would give her a chance to live another day. She could run. Go back to Aveline, pack their bags, and be on the next boat to Riven.

She crawled on her elbows, dragging her chest through the mud and grass. The sticks and thorns scraped against her arms. The broken foliage left a trail, but the gamble had been placed. Her heart pounded in her ears. No amount of deep breathing could clear the sound, muffling the noise of the forest around her. A rock sliced through the leg of her pant, drawing blood along the way. She swallowed her scream and blinked away the tears.

Inching backwards she found the sharp sliver of obsidian. Fragile yet deadly. The dirt caked beneath her fingernails, as she dug through the dirt around the glass, loosening it from the earth. It wasn't much longer than her hand, a pale replacement to the long thin blades buried in the back of a dying swine.

The squish of mud came from her right. She rolled away from the noise, popping into a low crouch.

Her right hand gripped the makeshift blade. Her left slid onto her pouch, feeling the three remaining vials left inside. She pulled out two of them, pinching one between her fingers and keeping the other pressed in her palm.

Another slurp of mud and this time she spotted the shift of a shadow to match it.

The first bottle left her hand as she flung it towards the movement. Ducking and rolling away from the explosion of purple flames she held her breath. She didn't close her eyes in time, the blinding flash of fire stealing her sight as the heat washed over her. Glancing back, she was too late. The shadow charged her. She hurled the second vial. Her pursuer twirled out of its way.

Renata pushed herself to her feet. A force hit her from behind. Arms wrapped around her waist. The two dove to the ground. Renata shifted in her attacker's grip. She drove the obsidian forward and into flesh.

The attacker gasped a single word. "Renia?"

And Renata's heart froze.

The first time Aveline called her Renia, her entire world softened. It was the perfect name for her new life. The name of a faithful lover, not of a knife-worn killer. They laid together in the bed, curled up against one another drenched in sweat.

"Why Riven? What is it you're running from?" Aveline asked. "How far will you go?"

With that, Renata tensed, pulling away from Aveline's touch.

After a moment of silence Renata sat up, grabbing her clothes from the floor.

"No." Aveline's hand hovered above Renia's. "I'm sorry. I thought . . ."

"I will never speak of it. You will never know. Every day the questions will dig at you. Every day it will drive a knife deeper between us. This was a lovely dream for a few nights but . . ."

"Please." Aveline pleaded. "Dunna worry. You won't believe me when I say I'm running too. We could both start new. Here. There's a farm for sale not far from here. The past is past. Just today, and tomorrow, and the next matter."

Renia turned and looked at Aveline, her eyes brimming with tears. "Your past?"

Aveline closed her eyes. "The world is filled with darkness. I'm done addin' to it. You though, it's like you're my guiding light forward."

Renia dropped her clothes and laughed. Her, a light? After everything she had done. After every life she had taken. "If I'm a light, you must be the sun."

"My light?" Aveline gasped as she collapsed. Her eyes went wide, her pupils dilated.

Renata rolled Aveline to her back and pulled a poultice from her belt, unscrewing the cap. The foul-smelling grease only added to the pain she felt. "I'm sorry. I'm sorry..." she repeated under her breath. She blinked her eyes hard again and again until her vision returned.

Renata pulled the black glass from Aveline's shoulder and pressed her weight onto the wound. High enough it should have missed anything vital. Low enough it was still a risk. "Aveline, you should be home."

"I had to put my past to rest." Her voice barely broke a whimper from the pain.

The warm blood seeped between Renia's fingers. She freed a hand, dipping her fingers into the poultice, and slathered the wound.

Aveline cried out.

"I'm sorry, my sun." Renia whispered.

"No, I am . . ."

They waited in silence for the bleeding to stop, gingerly tending to each other's wounds. Decades of questions gone unanswered no longer needed explaining. They sat holding each other's hands, their foreheads pressed together.

"We can't go back." Renia closed her eyes and squeezed Aveline's hands. "They know where to find us. Our house. Our lives."

Aveline returned the motion. "There's nothing there that canna be replaced."

"There's the quilt I made you for our anniversary four years ago."

"You can make it anew."

"And the chair you carved me beside the fire."

"The next will be better."

"Aveline . . ."

A finger pressed against Renia's lips. "Riven, wasn't it? Let's see what's there. You, my star, are all I need. The past doesn't matter."

Renia kissed the finger before brushing it aside and finding Aveline's lips with her own. "Just today, tomorrow, and the next."

ADVENTURE AWAITS

Rashelle Yeates

I stood at my bedroom window staring outside, at the bright sun and the clear blue sky that promised a perfect day. Outside. Where I wanted to be. Not stuck in the house visiting with a man I'm not interested in. My parents want me to marry him because he is the son of father's good friend, the Headman. They didn't say so in as many words, but they invited him over every time with his parents while not inviting any of their other sons.

"Ain Bel," mother's voice came through the door as it opened, "aren't you ready yet? We are all waiting on you."

She stood in the doorway her narrowed eyes searching the room until they stopped on me by the window. "What are you doing? We've been waiting for you for the longest while. Is something amiss?" Two steps. The farthest she's ever entered my room. Mother wasn't one to offer help. Celeste and I always had to go to her when we needed something. And my younger sister went to her with everything.

I wished Celeste was the elder. Then my parents wouldn't be so focused on me and what they had pictured for my future. what they wanted as my future. I tried so many ways to get them to focus on Celeste her instead of me, but they were adamant that I was the eldest. Every time I talked to Celeste she – ironically enough – didn't want to offend and wouldn't say anything to our parents.

All my life I wasn't allowed to make my own decisions. My

mother even decorated my room. I much preferred the greens and browns of my father's office to the pinks and whites my room was decorated with, even the dress I wore was decreed by my mother. I cast a quick look at the large wooden chest in the corner. It contained all I wanted. My parents thought it held the items for starting a new life – and it did – just not the life they expected me to have.

"No, nothing's wrong." Except everything was wrong, and although my mother would listen the answer was always what my father wanted.

"Then why are you up here staring out the window instead of downstairs with the rest of the family?" My mother huffed, her lips twisted up in an expression I saw a lot of lately.

"Why are we having them to breakfast?" I took a few short steps toward the door with the hope she would actually tell me the truth.

"The Headman and your father have business matters to discuss," she lied, "and breakfast was the only time they both had available." She walked out the door at a speed I refused to keep up with.

"If it's a business breakfast why are his wife and son coming? And why do we have to be there?" I muttered the words as I walked down the hall to the stairs, mother nowhere in sight. From the bottom of the stairs, I heard their conversation as I approached.

"Ain Bel's on her way."

"She'd better behave herself during breakfast."

Startled, I missed the next step, my feet tangling with each other and catching on the edge of the steps, hands grasping at the banister until I stopped half hanging over it. My father stood just inside the entry to the dining area and mother waited at the bottom of the stairs. The look on mother's face was one I hadn't seen before, and I never wanted to see it again. I didn't want to add anymore strange looks to the list.

I straightened, tossed my braid over my shoulder, and calmly continued making my way down the rest of the stairs. I stopped at the bottom waiting for my parents' criticism, since they always had one.

"I'm glad you didn't do that in front of everybody," my father's voice dripped with cold displeasure. "What kind of impression would that have made?"

I waited, watching my father, as a response from me wasn't required. They weren't the ones they tried to brainwash me with, so anything else wasn't the right ones.

As I continued to stare at my father he grunted and turned away. "So glad you finally deigned to join us. Try not to embarrass the family or make a fool of yourself this time."

"You better behave," mother hissed and grabbed my arm with bruising force to lead me into the room.

I pulled against her grip, not expecting to get free, but caught up as we got closer to the door. Being dragged into the room wasn't ideal.

Mother dropped my arm when we got to the door with a disbelieving glint in her eyes. "I'm so sorry for the delay." She announced moving around the table to take her seat at the opposite end.

I made my way to the seat next to Balard and across from Celeste without looking at the others. I flopped into my seat, my eyes on the table, and hands clenched in my lap. A grin tried to break free at the frustrated huff mother tried to suppress. It drew my eyes up to see Celeste pressing a napkin to her mouth. I couldn't tell if she was laughing at me or completely appalled by my behavior. Her eyes pleaded with me not to cause problems.

The servants brought out plates piled with the foods always served to the Headman and his family, breaking the tense silence following my entrance. It didn't surprise me that Celeste and I were the only ones to thank those serving us.

My goal is to survive another unbearable breakfast. , Once we started eating I scooped food into my mouth as quickly as possible. I wanted to finish as fast as possible until a comment from my mother caused my fingers to go slack, my fork clattering loudly against my plate.

"What?" I blurted looking at her with wide incredulous eyes. "What did you just say?"

Mother took her time to reply, dabbing at the corner of her mouth before placing her napkin in her lap and straightening her fork next to her plate. "We were discussing the wedding plans."

"Wedding plans?" My hand clenched, hovering over my plate. "What wedding plans?"

My other hand clenched in my lap at my mother's sigh. "We need to get started on the planning if you and Balard are going to be married in the style you deserve. I hadn't thought you would be interested in the details."

I stared at her, then Celeste's face caught my attention. There was guilt and something more, but I didn't have time to figure it out. I'd known there was more to this breakfast meeting than the business my father needed to discuss.

"I don't recall any marriage being proposed." Taking a deep breath, I looked down at my plate and picked up my fork so my mother wouldn't see the anger burning inside me.

"As I said," she retorted, a sharp bite to her tone, "I did not think you would be interested."

My eyes jumped to her face disbelieving her words. As if I wouldn't be interested in the fact that my parents were planning my marriage to Balard, all without talking to me about it. I knew they wanted the connection to the Headman and his family, but to do *this*. How could they? My teeth ground together trapping the words I wanted to lash out with behind them. I knew better than to do so, not with the Headman and his family here. Father would find new and inventive ways of punishing me if I let my growing fury out in front of them.

Mother caught my eye with a raised brow, knowing exactly what kept me silent. I gave her a toothy grimace back. It fooled no one. Another tense moment passed while our eyes did battle Abruptly, before mother turned back to Balard's mother to discuss plans I didn't plan on following through on.

Dressed comfortably I sat on the windowsill and contemplated the chest in the corner of my room. If I had my way, by tonight it'd be emptied.

Breakfast lasted well into the morning with me only being able to hear a few of the things my father discussed with the Headman. It was all a ruse. A way for my parents to force me to follow their decision.

They would be disappointed.

After all, I wasn't Celeste.

I wasn't the good girl who followed my parents orders. They should know better than to think that discussing wedding plans with the Headman's wife, in front of everybody would get me to go through with it. Doing that kept the angry words trapped behind my teeth, but it wouldn't get me to agree. It did, however, enforce my decision to leave.

I wouldn't be able to meet with Rupert until after the midday meal. My parents never looked for me until right before dinner. I didn't know – and didn't care – what they thought I was doing, as long as they didn't interfere.

I tugged at the cuffs of the long-sleeved tunic I wore. I was going mad waiting to go to the hidden vale where I practiced with Rupert. The only place we had where no judging eyes saw.

A light tapping on the door drew me from my circling thoughts. There was only one person who knocked so politely.

"Come in, Celeste."

Celeste pushed open the door poking her head through the opening. "How are you dealing with the news?"

"How do you think I'm dealing with it?" I pushed off the sill, pacing across the room with silent angry steps.

"I told Mother that she should tell you before breakfast. It was obvious to everyone that you didn't know anything about it." Celeste's white knuckled grip on the edge of the door showed her nervousness. It looked as if she wanted to use it as a shield.

"So, everyone knew what this breakfast was for except me?" I held my temper since my sister wasn't at fault. She was who she was. She followed the dictates of our parents like it was law. If she had been told not to tell me what was going on, she wouldn't have.

Celeste swallowed audibly. "Mother said it was better if you found out that way. Otherwise, you would have done something crazy."

"She does know me." I bit off a harsh laugh. "But not that well if she thinks I'm going to fall into line with their plans."

"Ain Bel," Celeste came the rest of the way into the room. "What are you planning?"

"I'm not planning anything."

"Yes, you are. You always have something going on in that crazy brain of yours."

I waved a hand through the air brushing aside the words. There were no plans, not yet, I had to talk to Rupert before any plans were made.

"Did you listen to any of what mother was discussing?" Celeste sat on the chest at the end of the bed.

So, Celeste wanted to talk.

It would keep my mind occupied until after the midday meal. And Celeste was better to talk to when our parents weren't around.

"No, why?" I made myself comfortable on the sill, my back to the glass to be warmed by the sun.

"They want the wedding to take place in the fall with the festival."

I feared I would break my teeth with how hard I clenched them. "That's only a month away."

"Exactly." Celeste raised her hands pleadingly. "This is your life, Ain Bel. You have to accept that you can't change it. Not with any of the shenanigans you've pulled. This is bigger than that."

"I'm not going to stop. I'm meant for so much more than just being Balard's wife." I shuddered at the horrible thought. Not thinking about Celeste in the room I mumbled, "I can't marry him."

"Can't? What do you mean can't?"

My eyes jumped to Celeste's. "Forget you heard that."

"No, I won't, Ain Bel. I don't want you to do something crazy and end up in a worse situation."

"I can't think of anything worse than marrying Balard. He's a bully, petty, and mean. You've seen him around his brothers." I refused to mention Rupert. Celeste might let his name drop and I wanted to keep him away from this.

"I've seen him." Celeste's mouth puckered in distaste. "But Father and Mother have decided, and they won't change their minds. I knew you would be unhappy with it. I did try to tell them, Ain Bel. They won't hear it."

"I know you tried." I looked out the window, wanting this discussion over with. The words of rebellion wanted to tumble off the end of my tongue like they have a thousand times before to my younger sister, but this time was different. I couldn't give them a voice just yet. They meant too much.

"Ain Bel, talk to me." Celeste tensed, waiting for words I wouldn't say. "Please."

"I've nothing to say Celeste." I looked back at my sister, wondering if this would be the last time we talked. She was poised delicately, looking at me with wide eyes. Suddenly I worried for her own future as well. "You know you don't have to do everything they tell you either."

"They are my parents, Ain Bel." Celeste retorted, frowning at me, "They deserve my respect and obedience."

It was an old argument, one that I could get lost in and forget about the time.

Leaning on one of the giant trees that stood sentinel around the hidden vale where Rupert and I practiced I checked the placement of the sun. The grass lay trampled from our practices, we couldn't always get away from our family obligations, but we still met more days than not. I hoped that this day wasn't one of those days Rupert couldn't get away because I wanted to talk to him about what happened at breakfast. I hoped that

Rupert was unaware of the true purpose of the breakfast that morning. My mind whirled with the different scenarios of what I would do if he knew and didn't tell me. Best friends shouldn't keep secrets like that from each other.

Being the youngest son of the Headman, Rupert wasn't as important as his five older brothers. Which meant he often wasn't normally privy to those kinds of decisions. That had to be the case.

"Aib," Rupert's light tenor drew my attention to the far side of the vale, where he walked into the sunshine with a wide smile on his face. "You beat me here, again. I thought I might be first this time."

I stared at him with my arms folded and no smile or return greeting.

"Did you know?"

He stopped in the middle of the vale. "No, I didn't know. I would have told you if I had. I found out at the midday meal."

"Your parents kept it quiet?" I moved to meet him in the dappled patch of sunlight that made it through the canopy. I aimed for his nose.

He ducked back, my fist just missing his face, the blue highlights in his black hair glinted with his movement. Hands up in defense, Rupert took a step back. "Hey, no need for that."

I grinned at him. My feet moved moving in the way he taught me. I wished my extra height gave me an advantage, but he was too quick and out of the way every time. That speed was something I wanted to emulate, but my body didn't move in the same way.

"Oh, it's like that is it?" He asked while dancing out of the way again, the grin back on his face, and not once attacking back. "Let me know when you get tired enough to talk about it."

The sun had moved quite a distance in the sky before I took a step back and lowered my hands. Not once had I connected with Rupert, his speed dizzying. How disappointing. I trained hard with him to improve my fighting skills, but he always was a step ahead.

"Do you feel better now that you've gotten that out of your system?" He stood back hands on hips, breathe only slightly labored.

"How do you do that?" I demanded, hands braced on my knees with my head hanging low. I felt like I had ran miles.

"I've practiced my whole life. You've only been practicing the last few years. Not that it'll do you much good after the fall."

I grimaced. He would have to bring up all those churning emotions and just when I got them settled so I could think clearly.

"You know Balard won't let you out of the house after you're married, right? He'd keep you under lock and key if he could get away with it."

"That's not going to happen."

"No, not to that extreme, but if you don't do what he wants you to, my parents will help restrain your movements until you learn your place."

"That's not what I meant." I straightened fighting down the panic that wanted to run riot. "I'm not going to marry him. I refuse."

"And your parents are fine with that?" Rupert reached down and pulled a thin bladed dagger from his boot, holding it aloft. "I think they would rather stab you with this than let you do what you want."

"Where did you get that? You didn't have it last time." I walked over and grabbed his wrist so I could examine the dagger more closely.

Rupert smiled, saying nothing until I let him go, finished with my inspection.

"Where do all our weapons come from?"

"That one's so nice I would think it would be missed."

"It might be, if the owner actually looks in the chest it was stored in."

"Rupert, I thought we agreed not to take anything from the villagers."

"The old man won't know it's missing. His children never come around and he spends his time in the chair outside his house. It was a simple in and out."

I swallowed the words I wanted to say. If Rupert agreed to my plan, it wouldn't matter if the old man noticed anyway.

"What are you thinking?" Rupert slid the dagger back into its sheath.

"I'm not going to marry Balard, Rupert. I can't. I just can't."

"That's all well and good, but it doesn't matter to anybody that has a say. Your parents want the match and so do mine." Rupert folded his arms, gaze unfocused, lost to his own thoughts. "I'm not sure why they want such a match. It would be better if Balard married someone from a neighboring town to strengthen trade and those connections."

"I never know what my parents are thinking. I wasn't even told about the marriage being planned until I heard it this morning." I paced away, my thoughts a chaotic jumble.

I didn't know how to start, but if I left it for too long Rupert would go home and the opportunity to ask him about leaving would be gone.

"I think it's how they plan to keep you in line. And Balard can be . . . difficult." Rupert waited, but when I didn't respond he moved into my path, forcing me to stop or walk through him. "Spit it out, Aib. What else has you all twisted up?"

Walking through him had never worked before so I stopped.

"What makes you think there's something more?" I couldn't bring myself to speak my hopes aloud. If I did and he didn't agree, then I would be on my own. I didn't want to do this without him.

"I know you. We've been friends for years. You already worked through your anger from this morning. What has you still wound so tight?" His folded arms said he wasn't going anywhere until he got an answer.

Scrubbing my hands over my face, I braced them on my hips, and blew out a breath. If I didn't speak now, I wouldn't have another chance. My chest constricted with the pressure of not knowing what his answer would be.

"I want us to Cat." The words came out strangled, getting caught somewhere in the middle of my throat.

"What?" Rupert dropped his arms and took a step closer. "Aib, what did you say?"

I took a deep breath, cleared my throat, and tried to sound confident. "I said, I think we should Cat."

"Cat?" Rupert made a sound I couldn't decipher. "We made that plan when we were kids."

I waited. I had thought about that long ago plan the whole morning. I wanted to give Rupert some time to think about it, but a quick glance at the position of the sun said we didn't have that kind of time.

"You really want to do this?" He asked after an excruciatingly long wait.

I raised my palms to the sky, "I won't marry Balard. I want to live my life the way I want to live it. Leaving is the only way that can happen. My parents will never allow me to do the things I want. Exploring is not an acceptable thing for their daughter to do. It's never going to change, not unless I do something to change it."

"Don't you think they'll be worried about you?"

"I think your parents will be the ones who are worried, but I can't live my life the way somebody else dictates anymore. This is what I want to do, so that's what I'm going to do. And I want you to do it with me."

"Just slink away in the middle of the night."

With that musing tone of voice I knew he wasn't talking to me. It sounded like he was intrigued but unsure. I wanted to give him more time, but his lapse into silence was unnerving. "Well? What are your thoughts?"

He looked over at me and for a wild moment I thought he would say no, until the huge smile took over his face. "Let's do it. I'm so ready to be a cat that slinks away out of sight. You think you're ready for that?"

An answering grin spread across my own face. "Just you wait,

I'm going to out eat you this time."

"No way." He laughed, delighting me with his happiness to join in. "If we're going to do this, we need to get back. We can't let anybody know what's going on. Especially not Celeste. I know she loves you, but her duty as a daughter comes first."

I nodded. It was the truth. If Celeste knew that we planned to leave, she would tell our parents. I wished I could confide in her so she wouldn't worry, but I couldn't take the chance of our parents finding out.

"Tonight then?"

Rupert, still grinning, nodded and pointed two fingers at me. "Tonight."

It was easy to keep everyone from knowing what I planned. Hiding behind the anger I felt for my parents trying to force an arranged marriage gave me an excuse not to talk to them when I got home.

The evening meal was a torturous affair. My father's displeasure in my attitude was obvious, creating tension throughout the group.

"What do you have to say for yourself?"

I choked down the bite of food I had in my mouth. "I don't know what you mean."

"Don't you?" He kept his attention focused on placing his fork next to his plate just so. "Why do you always have to be so difficult? Why can't you do as you're told?"

"Because I don't want this life." I blurted out, waving a hand at everything. "I want to live a life I choose to live."

I can't believe I said that. I've held in my anger and frustration for so long I couldn't do it anymore, it just burst out. I put a hand to my mouth, instantly regretting my words. My mother glared across the table, her anger boring into me. I hope I didn't give anything away.

My father's hard eyes caught mine refusing to let me look away. "You will obey."

I blinked. Did he think saying it again changed anything?

"You will conform," he emphasized again, "or you will no longer be a daughter of mine."

"What?" I whispered. The pinched look on my mother's face reflects the one I'd seen that morning. So that's what that look meant.

"I'm no longer your daughter if I don't do what you tell me to do?" I asked again, making sure I heard correctly.

"That is what I said. You will do as you are told. You will marry Balard or you will no longer be welcome in this house."

Celeste tried catching my eye through the rest of the meal, but I refused to engage. There was nothing to say. I wasn't welcome here anymore and no longer a part of this family. I pushed away from the table, ignoring my mother's demand that I come back and finish the meal.

I spent the rest of the night in my room, ignoring Celeste's knock at my door. There was nothing more to say. Not about what she came to talk about. I didn't want to hear the reasons why being a good daughter mattered. I wasn't a good daughter and didn't want to be if it meant not living the life I wanted.

Having set out my clothes before extinguishing the lamp for the night, I dressed smoothly in the dark. The trickiest part was finding the key to the locked chest at the end of my bed in the bottom of the armoire. Before panic had time to settle in my stomach my fingers felt the cool metal. I wrapped my hand tightly around it not wanting to lose my lifeline and end up needing to light a lamp.

I walked the few steps to the chest on silent feet and reached for the lock. My grip slipped and the key clanked against the metal. I paused, listening intently, to hear if the noise had disturbed anybody. All was silent in the house.

Leaving the key in the lock I lifted the lid. The hinges raised soundlessly like I knew it would because of my diligent oiling. Reaching in I grabbed the strap of the brown and black patterned pack sitting on top that was always at the ready.

Why had it taken so long to take this step? Rupert and I had planned this when we were children, but I never stopped being ready to go at a moment's notice. I didn't belong here. My father was right. This wasn't my home. Perhaps it never had been.

Hefting the pack to my shoulder, I made my way down the stairs, avoiding the areas that creaked, to the kitchen. Where I put together a small pack of food for the first part of our journey. We planned to hunt for food along the way, but I wanted to get far enough away from the village before taking the time for that.

I carefully laid the bag of food in the space I left at the top of the pack. There was more in the bag then I thought. I needed to rearrange the items to make it fit better, but I refused to light a lamp to do that.

I stopped at the outer kitchen door, hand on the handle, and looked back over my shoulder at the only home I knew. I felt a small knot of regret at leaving without telling Celeste goodbye.

That was it.

Shouldn't I feel more?

Shouldn't I feel something about leaving my parents? There was nothing. Just . . . nothing. Shaking my head, I pulled the door open knowing it wouldn't make a noise as it was well maintained.

My steps grew lighter and lighter the closer I got to the small cave where we cached the weapons. I didn't need a light to find the way because the moonlight shone with the brightness of a small torch.

Rupert stepped out of the cave, weapons in hand. Without a word he handed me the axe I was most familiar with.

"No problems?" I asked taking the weapon and affixing it to my belt. The weight felt awkward and heavy, but I knew it would become more familiar with time.

"None." He secured his own weapon to its spot.

"I thought there would be more."

"More what?" He asked, looking up from his task.

"I don't know." I shrugged. "More. . .something."

"Well, let's go find your more, Aib." Rupert grinned at me, the moonlight casting crazy shadows across his face.

I grinned back at him, "Thank you for coming with me. I don't know that I would have the gumption to go on my own."

"You would have." He assured me, taking my hand in a firm grip, his eyes locked on mine. "I'm happy to take this adventure with you. I'd go on any adventure – if it's with you."

I squeezed his hand to prevent him from pulling away and kept my eyes on his. "I wouldn't want to go on an adventure without you."

We stood staring into each other's eyes for a moment longer. Flustered, I pulled away, waving a hand for him to take the lead.

This wasn't what I expected, but not knowing what to expect was the point of adventure, wasn't it?

FATE AND KARMA MEET FOR COFFEE

Candace J. Thomas

Fate sat at a café table nested next to a small ornamental garden. A delicate breeze swept through her hair loosened from her penciled bun. She slowly sipped her coffee while watching a woman search her purse at the register.

"Keep searching," she whispered into her cup. "Just around your sunglasses." The woman pulled out a full punch card for a free lunch, a shocked expression covering her face. A quick crease raised from Fate's lips in a slight smile.

"Are you giving away lunch again?" a deep voice broke around the chattering conversations.

Fate lifted her gaze to Karma's sly grin as he plopped down in a chair at her table. Overly dressed in ostentatious fashion, slick and polished with his signature I have arrived attitude. A deep smell of cinnamon complimented his bright clothes and bright white smile. Fate couldn't help rolling her eyes at the spectacle.

Karma propped his feet like a footrest and eyed her coffee. "So, did you order one for me?"

"Does your conscience deserve one?" She took another sip.

Karma cracked his neck side to side. "Probably. I think you knew I'd show up."

A waitress appeared holding a small tray. "Sorry for the wait. Here you go." She placed the steaming cup before him.

"Thank you," Fate said to the waitress. The girl nodded and navigated her way back through the crowded tables.

Karma raised his eyebrows in mock surprise. "Well, I guess fate is smiling on me."

Fate's expression slid to a pensive simmer. "Drink up. You should be wide awake for this conversation."

"They're always stimulating, my dear." He took a deep draw of the coffee. "Whoo! That's the stuff. You added nutmeg, you little minx."

Fate put her coffee down and reached in her bag, pulling out a notebook. She let her fingers glide over the pages until she found a blank sheet. She took a pencil from her bun and started to draw.

Karma ogled her sketch. "Is this the girl?"

"Yes." She continued with a quick profile. "Her name is Sophie. She should be here . . . right about now." She pointed to the street corner with her pencil.

A young woman stood at the crosswalk fumbling with a pocket in her backpack. She shuffled along with the traffic of people as she slipped the straps around her back.

Karma analyzed the girl then glanced back to Fate's sketch. "You're good, and incredibly fast. I mean, you already have her nose."

Fate brushed away the shedding from her eraser. "Years of practice." She shaded in finer details then wrote the girl's name underneath. "There."

Karma hummed. "That's how they're sealed to you? You put them in a notebook?"

"Their fate isn't sealed to anything," Fate clarified. "It's simply drawn with a pencil. I can erase it if I need to." She shifted more toward him. "Desire and belief is more delicate an operation than whatever you do."

Karma shrugged. "I don't make the rules. I follow them."

Fate shifted focus to shading around the face and cars. "I have a hard time following rules."

"I'm aware of that," Karma huffed. "You're soliciting my

help. That's against the playbook." He took another glance toward Sophie as she entered the café. There was a kindness to her, a sweet temper with a question stuck in the upper crease in her smile. "I can see that this girl's not anyone on my list. So, tell me the problem."

"You might like this one." On the same page Fate started doodling a curling swoop of hair and thick frame glasses.

Karma guffawed. "Wait. That guy?"

"I've read them both, and they're perfectly matched."

Karma leaned in closer as Fate filled in freckles, an angled jaw, goofy expression.

"That's close." She scrolled the name Lucas under the sketch.

Karma shifted from one picture to the next. "She and him?" Another laugh bellied out of him.

Fate crossed her arms and sat back. "I don't find what's so amusing."

"I always wondered how some couples ended up together. This guy is not in her league."

"I promise they're soulmates."

"You're ridiculous." He took another swig of coffee.

Fate's fingers drilled up on her arms waiting. "You see now why I need your help."

"Well," Karma started, "I can see the hill you climb. This guy," reading from the page, "this Lucas has debt. Serious debt."

"Is that how karma works?"

Karma took a deep breath before continuing. "Sort of. There are consequences." He shook out a laugh like ringing bells.

Fate remained stoic amid his laughter. "Well, I don't operate the same as you."

Karma's eyes caught her. He moved slowly closer. "And yet, here we are," he stated before brushing each arm as if flicking off dust. "Tell me then, if you don't have rules how exactly does fate 'operate'?"

Fate leaned forward, placing her elbows on the table. She tapped her pencil unconsciously deliberating her thoughts. "Does everything need rules? Why should there be rules when it comes to fate?"

"It doesn't seem very fair. You're not playing the same game the rest of us are. Everyone here in this city is following rules, all the time. It's like getting something for nothing."

Fate squared up in her seat, clearly annoyed. "Those who believe pay a lot for that trust. You talk about fate like it doesn't have a cost."

"Well, it doesn't," Karma returned. "Fate is cosmic and mystical."

"Not true," Fate pointed out. "Being fated is only given to the faithful. Not everyone gets that chance." She pointed toward the line of patrons waiting to order. "In that whole line there, Sophie is the only one who believes in fate. A believer who has reserved her space for the right person. I can't deny her that. Fate is precious to these people. They recognize it when I'm there. Others don't. If you don't believe in fate, how can you understand when it happens?"

Karma pulled at his beard. "So, the cost for a believer is trusting the unfathomable belief that you'll someday cosmically collide with your person at some point and recognize it as fate?"

"Something like that," she replied. "Not many people believe I can do anything for them."

"Like my boyLucas here. He's not one to hold stock in the supernatural."

Fate tucked a stray hair behind her ear thinking of the unbelievers. "Well, I need to change that. Something supernatural should touch him."

"But you know I can't let him off that easily." Karma chuckled. "As I said, Lucas has debt. He'd get a free pass if you just wished him to meet her. I can't do that."

"And if he did good things, could he accrue good karma? That's how it works, right?"

Karma waffled. "Well, yes. But—"

Fate flattened out the adjacent page in her notebook. "Tell me about his debt."

Karma leaned back in his chair, resting his hands behind

his head milling over all the details. "How much do you know about him?"

Fate eyed her sketch feeling the details in the chin and gleam in his eyes. "Well, I know he's a college grad. NYU. Works with computers. Likes classic fantasy novels."

"You see?" Karma threw out his hands. "Right there. You listed a lot of the problems."

Fate halted. "What problems? By being a little brainy?"

"Too brainy."

Fate tsked. "That isn't fair."

"He's too smart, and it gets him in trouble. He gets bored. Hacks computer sites just because he can. He and a few of his college friends made computer viruses that attacked health care systems." Karma blinked with huge exaggeration. "I mean, health care systems. Who does that?"

Fate heaved a small breath. "That is a lot to weigh."

"And what about the gambling trip," he started, "where he lied to his mother and consequently blew all his college savings. And then borrowed money from his grandfather to cover up that lie." Karma rocked his head. "You don't ever lie to your mother. Trust me, I know. Shani has never forgiven me." He shuddered at the memory.

"No need to bring up the past," Fate waved off what clearly looked unpleasant. "I do agree with you there."

Karma came closer. "Then there's Nick, his best friend from childhood. Nick leant Lucas his Tolkien books and Lucas kept them." He held up his hands. "He never gave them back. Claimed them as his."

"Really?" That's on your list of debt?" Fate questioned flatly. "It's possible Lucas didn't remember where they came from."

"No, he knows."

"So, he should give the books back?" Fate offered, scribbling it down on the list.

"Sounds too easy." Karma sat up straight and snapped his fingers. "And the kitten incident."

"A kitten?"

"Yeah, when he strapped a bottle rocket to a kitten."

Fate sat back in disbelief. "Was he a kid? I don't think you can count the actions of anyone under ten-years old. Now, if he was twenty and strapped bottle rockets to cats, that's a different story."

"Yeah, but kittens though."

"Did the kitten live?"

"Well, yes, but it never grew hair on its back from those burns."

Fate tapped her pencil. "I'm not counting that one."

"But all that other stuff. That's what I mean by Debt, with a capital D."

"I hear what you're saying," Fate stated, weighing the options. "But all you see is debt. You aren't factoring other good things that he's done."

"True. I haven't been reading the good Karma reports." Karma leaned in. "But it's not fair to have this boy skip out on all that." He went back and drained the last of his cup. "Whoo. That was good." He crushed the paper cup and shot it like a basketball toward the garbage, hitting it dead center. "Yes! You know I get three points for that, right?"

Fate simpered a smile. "So, back to my deal. I need Lucas. For my magic to work, it has to be him."

"And this Sophie's so perfect for him?"

"Yes." Fate examined her drawing. "Sophie has a really good heart. That's one of the reasons why she's good for Lucas. Sophie needs a friend to believe in her, but also someone to believe in as well. Someone funny. Someone that understands her geek style and affinity for cat paraphernalia. Someone she can stay up late with just talking."

"I don't know," Karma hummed. "Doesn't seem like enough."

Fate leaned over and touched his knee. "Love, true love, is not something that is fleeting, it's a lasting gift. These two have a chance for that, a chance that we didn't get. I don't want to see anyone else be placed in a situation where they no longer have that gift. If any of my believers have a chance for it, something that will glow forever, I want to see it and recognize it. I don't want anyone to wait until it is too late."

Karma slipped his hand on hers before lifting it to his lips. He closed his eyes and sighed. "I remember," he whispered into her fingers. "I think of that chance every day."

"Then let it happen here for these two."

Karma pulled Fate's hand to his chest before letting it go. He glanced again at the doodle of Lucas and then back at the real Sophie, who now sat at a tiny table alone picking at a little salad while reading. "I don't think this guy deserves her."

"I can't predict the future, so I don't know how things end. I do know that never was there so perfect an arrangement than these two." Her hand slipped tenderly to Karma's arm. "They have a chance. Even someone with a debt like his deserves to find a soulmate. So, what kind of arrangement can we strike?"

Karma took her fingers and kissed them again. "You always give people chances, don't you?"

"I give them a choice," Fate clarified. "I arrive at the very apex in their pathway, and they can choose. I believe in their actions, their choice."

Karma rubbed her hand. "Fine. You got me. But let's say in a few years, I'm cashing in. Make him get a cat or rescue kittens."

Fate jotted it down, permanently inking the reminder in the timeline of life. "Fair."

"But it's not gonna be all sunshine." Karma jabbed his finger at the drawing. "That virus stuff can't be dismissed. He can't run away from that."

"Sophie can help him"

"It might stress their relationship."

"Or make it stronger." She wrote down more notes. "Anything else?"

Karma winced a little. "Well, I think it might be good for him to have daughters."

Fate let out a gentle laugh. "All daughters?"

"No, but a daughter or two will repay his debt completely." Karma slapped the table. "Okay. I'm satisfied."

Fate lit up with a smile. "Fantastic." She finished her last note. "Because he's due to arrive here any moment."

Karma looked around. "Where?"

Fate pointed at the east corner of the streetlight. "It's his lunch break. He usually brings his lunch, but he was late this morning and forgot it at home."

Karma found Fate's drawing in real life waiting at the crosswalk. He glanced back to where Sophie had eaten her lunch. She was now standing grabbing her backpack and pushed her book in the side pouch before hauling it on her back. "Wait. She's leaving."

Lucas had already crossed the street by now.

Karma threw his arms in her direction. "She's walking away. She's gonna miss him."

Fate smiled. "Not this time." She drew a tiny heart between the two sketches and closed her notebook.

Sophie's book fell to the ground right before where Lucas walked. He quickly picked it up. Together Fate and Karma watched as he stooped to pick it up.

"Hey. You dropped this."

Sophie turned to see him. "Oh, thank you."

Lucas looked at the book. "Oh, wow. I have this copy of The Hobbit."

Sophie smirked. "Really? It's rather old, but I liked the art in it."

"Oh, me too. My friend lent me his copy when I was a kid." He smiled at the memory. "Huh, I should probably get it back to him."

Sophie checked out the cover. "I think this was my mom's copy."

"That's really cool."

The moment quieted.

"Well," Sophie grasped her book tight in her hands. "Thanks." She turned and started walking down the sidewalk away from Lucas.

Karma met Fate's gaze. "He's letting her go." He stood, panicked as he watched Sophie walk away.

Fate came around him placing her arm through his. "I can only create the moment, Karma. They have to decide, remember?"

Karma made hand gestures like he could push Lucas forward. "Go! Get her! You won't find her again. Don't lose this."

Lucas stood staring.

"Are you becoming a believer?" Fate stared at Karma with a satisfied smile.

Karma patted her arm and looked on, not answering her question.

. . .

"Wait!" Lucas shouted.

Sophie glanced back.

"You, ah . . ." Lucas stumbled for words. "You wanna grab lunch? I'm heading to lunch." He thumbed over his shoulder.

"Ah, I just ate."

"Coffee?" Lucas rushed.

Sophie tucked her hair behind her ear. "Ah, sure. I could get a coffee."

"I'm Lucas, by the way."

"Sophie."

"Grab a table. I'll, ah, go get some coffee."

Lucas sidled into the street café and got in line.

Sophie scouted a vacant table near the corner of the café. A particularly lovely spot, shaded by a cherry blossom tree. A peculiar sensation wrapped around her like wind, something distantly familiar, yet completely unknown. She turned, feeling as if someone was watching her, but she saw no one. Her only company was a fresh hint of cinnamon in the air.

A FUTURE TOLD

Logan Sidwell

I saw the quartz lose its sheen. For the first time, something was happening. A chill air flooded my lungs, but when I searched for a source, there was nothing. Just a red table, covered in crystals, and an enveloping purple curtain. I wish I could say the books were a help, but outside of big ideas, there was very little they agreed on. I figured the best I could do was focus my mind and let things happen.

I inhaled slowly, holding that cold wind inside while counting down. The room seemed unchanged. There was still that wrinkle in the fabric on the corner of the table. Every crystal lay in its proper place, equidistant and gently curving. A gradient of colors all pointed towards the middle, amplifying my signal to the cosmos. I released my breath and leaned closer to the quartz.

I had found it just a few hours earlier, tumbling down a long hill only to stop at my feet. I knew it was special from the moment I saw its bold translucence. Now carefully set on my table, the stone was misty, filled with a flowing gray vapor. I reached out, but stopped myself. Best not to interfere when things were finally happening.

I brought my attention back to the center of the table, the meeting place of every stone's energy. Atop a cheap metal framework sat the ball, a cloudy sphere smaller than my fist. It was just my reflection staring back at me. Nothing special. I never liked that crystal ball, it always seemed too small. But every time I asked about the big ones, someone would laugh and say a glass ball was good for nothing but starting fires.

Wait, my reflection? I paused, my eyes locked onto the image of my own brown eyes. My nose dragged long down my face, my eyes squinted out from behind a pair of thick rim glasses, and my tousled black hair hung a little carelessly past my eyebrows. I had stared into this thing a hundred times, and the only vision I had ever had was of the curtains on the other side of the room.

I'm not sure how much time passed as we stared out at one another, but for the longest time, I was motionless. I suppose I didn't say anything because I was waiting for him. I had spent six years reaching out to the cosmos, and for all of it, the cosmos had been mute. I felt the urge to laugh and cry at once. Not only had I managed to establish communication with the future, but in my divine flailings, I had dialed myself.

"It's you."

He spoke with a western lilt. I could hardly keep myself from smiling, it was my own scratchy voice. Soon the thrill in my heart grew too large to contain.

"It's me."

In those few words, we were bonded. He smiled, I smiled back, and we both relaxed into our chairs. With his face no longer blocking the view, I saw past him and into his home. The place looked run-down, hardly more than a shack. Warped wood walls barely blocked the wind. Aged, dusted desks looked mounted to the walls. And above them, basic tools everywhere. Well-worn saws, hammers, shovels, and many more I didn't recognize were all coated in tan dirt. Between the faded cracks at the edge of the crystal, I could just make out a window. It was nothing but wilderness beyond the glass.

"So," he started, "Whatcha gonna teach me?"

It was precisely the question I had intended to ask of him. "Teach you? I'm sorry—I thought you would be teaching me." His face fell at my answer. My nervous excitement started to fade.

The man spoke again. "Pardon me, I—I just caught a glance of your housing there and jumped the gun a little." His eyebrows raised apologetically, and his shoulders hunched over. I wondered if that was how I looked when I apologized. But more than that, I was disappointed. I had been looking for a guide, someone to point me towards the right way of living, someone with the benefit of a century of hindsight. But this didn't seem to be him. Was there something here I was overlooking?

He looked lost and disappointed, I realized how poorly I had hid my feelings.

"That's all right. It's really no problem! I wish I could explain why the two of us were connected to one another, but I just don't have the answers. It seems pretty clear that we're- Well, we're . . ."

"One and the same," he answered.

"Right, one and the same," I said with a slight smile.

"What do ya go by?"

"Drew."

The man let out an ugly, snorting laugh, just like mine. "Never heard that name, Drew. Kinda strange." I could see him chuckling to himself. I couldn't help but feel a little self-conscious. Was my name really so odd?

"I guess it is a little strange. What's yours?"

A bright smile stuck to his face as he spoke. "Oh, I have a good, solid name. Andrew."

At that moment, I got the joke and started to chuckle.

From the boxes of divining crystals and used up candles in the back of Andrew's room, I could tell the two of us shared a very similar journey. He had probably called out to other dimensions for years, just like me, and in the end, we had both ended up finding someone with our own face and name. I think we could both feel something more than even kinship between us, and for a while, in the face of the extraordinary, we laughed.

Once we talked more, I determined a few things. Rather than contacting the future, I had made a connection with the past, a little over a hundred years. With a bit of online research,

I was able to find Andrew's name on an old engineer's manifest from the early nineteen-hundreds. The moment I found his scrawled name halfway down a page, I dropped my phone and looked back at him. "You're real."

"No kiddin'. We related?" Andrew asked.

"I don't think so. But at the same time, how can we be anything less than brothers?" We both smiled at that. We asked about each other's lives. I don't think Andrew ever quite understood what my job was, but we eventually landed on the word accountant. It didn't quite capture the intricacies of Business Strategy and Statistical modeling, but his ears sure perked up when I told him I worked from home each day. "No meetin' with the boss? No runnin' to the bank? No nothin'?"

I nodded my head, and Andrew pressed me for more. When I had told him all I could, he sat back. "Well, ain't you blessed! I gotta wake up with the sun and run machines till light's out everyday."

Seeing someone so amazed at my work and the position I had put myself in gave me an ounce of pride. It had been a long time since I had felt anything like that about my life. I glanced away from the western scene to my own space. I had a hardwood floor, a wide area to live and bathe in, and no matter the weather, things were always comfortable—not like those sudden winds that picked up and rattled Andrew's home every couple of hours. It was an extraordinarily lucky way to live.

Since meeting Andrew, I had wondered why we had been connected, wondered if he could somehow guide me to a better life. Now it was clear. I wasn't here to be shown the way. I was here to give my doppelganger a better life. A safer one, like mine.

"Andrew?" I asked.

"Hmm?"

"I've been thinking, and it occurs to me . . . I hope I'm not imposing, but I was thinking I might be able to help you out." The words caught in my throat a little as I said them. Was my offer an insult? Was I implying his life was somehow lesser than mine? Andrew stayed deep in thought for a minute, leaving me to stew in my own worries. Suddenly his eyes opened wide,

"Oh, I see! You could show me one or two things from your time and I could make a copy of it, sell it far and wide. And hey! I could set you up too! Bury somethin' and show you where it is. We could both get out of this with a mint! Whaddya think?"

There are some ideas that, by speaking them, collide with an unwritten code. Somewhere deep inside my soul, Andrew's idea felt wrong. Just his words repelled me like the voicing of a taboo. A law carved into our very nature. I didn't want to tell him no, but there was no way I would do it. The air felt heavy, and I could see Andrew struggling with something similar in his own eyes. Finally, he spoke. "Drew, mayhaps—It's better we just appreciate a good thing," he gestured at his crystal ball, "for what it is, rather than goin' and makin' a killin' off it."

The heavy tension that held the air diffused. Inside, I was just happy I wasn't the one that had to say it. "I think you're right. We shouldn't try to change the world. But maybe we could change each other. I could teach you. Show you how I live."

"I like the sound of that, but—" Andrew turned away from the crystal ball, and I could see out the window the once bright scene had faded to total black. "Time's up for me. I hope we find each other again, but if we don't . . . It's been a pleasure."

"We could give it another go tomorrow, 6PM?" I asked. Andrew raised his hands, showing his wrists to me, "I ain't quite got the grasp of time you do, so you'll have to give me some leeway"

"Sure thing. Have a good night." Andrew nodded and waved. I reached for my cloudy quartz, attempting to disrupt the connection. As my fingers wrapped around the sharp edges, a stinging pain struck my hand, and a yelp came through from the other side of the crystal. I dropped the quartz and shouted, "Are you okay?"

I could hear a few mutterings on the other side, but nothing I could make out. Slowly, Andrew sat back in his chair, cradling a bloodied index finger. "Oh I'm fine. Just had a bite taken out of me by some quartz."

Raising my hand, I saw a thin trail of blood trickling down my digit into the palm. "So did I."

I could see Andrew's injury very nearly matched mine. The same finger, nearly the same cut. The two of us shared a look. Whatever it meant, we could tell it was significant. There was a bond here deeper than a face and a name, but just how close were we tied? With a grave expression, Andrew said, "You be careful."

"I will." I carefully extended my uninjured arm towards the quartz, and using the back of my palm, pushed it out of alignment. Slowly, the image of my own face, caught in a dark look, faded into the curtains of my apartment.

With Andrew gone, I quickly found the seam in my curtain and rushed for the sink. I washed, cleaned, and bandaged my finger quickly. For half the night, I couldn't sleep, thinking about Andrew, about the meaning of it all, and about that pulsing pain in my wrapped finger.

I waited a little too long before attempting the ritual the next night. When Andrew's face appeared on the other side, it was bathed in the last light of evening. "You made it back."

"I'm sorry I'm late."

Andrew shook his head. "I'm sure you did your best. With what time you have, can you teach me somethin'?"

I had made a lot of notes. Andrew was patient, but I still shuffled through the pages like there was a ticking clock. As soon as I saw the first word of the page I was looking for, all its contents flooded my brain. "Here it is!" I pulled the page free and placed it on my desk. "I know time is tight, but I wanted to talk about your work."

"Course. Whaddya wanna know?"

I hesitated. If it had been presumptuous to offer my guidance before, what I was about to say could come across as downright rude. "There's a lot of smoke in the factory you work at, isn't there?"

"Sure is," he said with a nod.

"The smoke is toxic. If you keep breathing it every day, it will kill you."

Andrew's brow furrowed. He looked right at me, and I knew that expression. Doubt. "I appreciate what yer tryin' to do, Drew, but I can handle a cough. Lotta folks have worked there a lot longer than I have. And I sure haven't seen anyone keel over lately."

"No." I shook my head, "You wouldn't. In fact, there's no guarantee you would even die, but statistically, for every day you spend breathing that stuff in—" I could see I had lost Andrew somewhere around "statistically." Carcinogens were such a complex thing. I tried again. "The poison's slow acting, and it's not just in the smoke. It's the dust you touch, probably the food you eat, everything. If you quit now, you might survive."

Andrew rubbed his thumb and middle finger together, a bit of grime washing away. "Did ya—Do you know for sure?" I knew what he was asking, and I had thought about it.

"No, I didn't want to know when you died." Talking to Andrew, he felt like a real person, someone from today, just on the other side of the world. I had nearly looked it up once, but I was afraid that if I looked him in the eye again after I knew, he'd suddenly be a memory.

"I got a bit saved. 'Nuff to travel, get me by for a few months. But I don't know what I need to, to do somethin' else." He sounded hopeless, but that's why I was here, wasn't it?

"I can help you! Without your job, you'll have more time, and I can teach you some of the things I do."

"Banker's work, really?"

"Absolutely, you already know you can do it!" I pointed at myself and he smiled.

"S'pose I do." I could see Andrew nodding to himself, building himself up. "It's a deal! You teach me and I'll be the best student you've ever seen!"

Maybe this was my calling? To be a teacher, help lift others to my level. I tried my best to reflect Andrew's energy. "Tomorrow I'll get you started on mathematics, but tonight, let's talk about your living situation."

Andrew took to my ideas fast. Whatever writing he had learned when he was young was more than enough to get through my lectures. In days he was already working through multiplication tables while I was figuring out what precisely he needed to know to become an accountant.

At the same time, I had managed to convince him to redecorate his house. During one session, I noticed there was no longer a torrent of wind when we connected, and he showed me the rescaling he had done on the windows and panels. He had even started talking about finding something like the incense I always burned during sessions.

"It's strange." During one of our lulls, Andrew spoke to me freely. "There were all sorts of things that always felt wrong to me. Dirt on my fingers, coughin' through every shift, walking up and down those rickety trails. But talking to you, it feels like everything makes a little more sense. I'm not s'posed to be outside all the time. I'm not s'posed to be walkin' near cliff edges and livin' in a shack that lets in the wind. Lately, it's been feelin' like I'm living the way my body's s'posed to live. Free of danger, ya know?"

I nodded along. "You're getting it now. There is a reason I work from home, Andrew. You and I are living in different, but equally deadly worlds. If you can minimize that risk every day, well, I think that's the best way to live longer."

Andrew wrote down everything I said, then glanced out the window. "Time's up again. Tomorrow afternoon good for you?"

"It's good for me," I said.

"Good, I got some new supplies rollin' in. Can't wait to show you."

After checking the doors, the windows, and the alarms, I went to bed feeling accomplished. It was new for me, but I loved it. I played out every word Andrew and I had said during the lecture, patting myself on the back for every good question he asked and every good answer he gave. It was wild. Just three weeks ago, I had been searching for direction, believing I was a lost soul struggling for purpose and connection. Finding Andrew had shown me just how wrong I was. With a little nudge from my philosophies, I had changed a person's world. And when I was finished here, who's to say I couldn't do it again?

The next afternoon, I re-entered my little ritual chamber and began the focussing process. It all took longer than usual. I grew impatient as I tried to focus on the ball at the table. Eventually, the quartz clouded over, and the ball revealed a scene on the other side.

The first thing that struck me was the smell. A heavy, flowery odor that crashed across my senses and left me dizzy. Andrew was there, though I couldn't see much more than his hair draped over the desk. There was shrill beeping behind me for just a moment, giving me a terrible headache.

I was pretty sure it was Andrew, but the whole scene was confusing. Instead of the standard wood walls and windows, there was a purple curtain, just like mine—maybe a little darker and more textured. I struggled to get my thoughts together and shouted through to the other side. "Andrew! Wake up!"

From what I could see, there was no movement. The blood drained from my face as something about the scene struck me the wrong way. "Andrew! Are you all right?" My voice echoed through my apartment, but there was no response.

Leaning close to the ball, I strained my eyes to see more detail. Was he breathing? It didn't look like it. My own chest felt like it was rising and falling much faster than usual. I scanned the area for blood. Nothing. I screamed Andrew's name again and again. Seeing my own face, motionless, probably lifeless on the other side, my stomach churned. Eventually, my voice gave out, my head lulled from side to side, and it felt strangely light and heavy, all at once.

He was dead. I was as certain as I could be. I leapt to my feet and backed towards the curtains. My arms flailed left and right searching for the opening. It felt like death was right there, reaching through the ball and closing in. Finally, my hand caught the edge of the fabric, and I threw myself through it.

Back in the cold mundanity of my apartment, I could barely breathe. The pounding in my head drifted away, and I started to catch myself. How had he died? There was nothing in the room to kill him. Everything about that scene was so unnatural. I thought back to our first encounter, when we had toyed with the idea of trading secrets from our respective times. Had he gone through with it? Had he crossed the great cosmic taboo and brought on divine retribution?

I thought again of the crystal ball, just on the other side of the curtain. It was still open to the gruesome scene on the other side. As much as I'd like to say I was thinking of Andrew in that moment, the first thought that came was simple. Could whatever have gotten Andrew be coming for me?

My mind was still a haze, but a part of me felt there was a terrible threat inching closer with every moment. I steeled myself and dashed back into my divining den. I averted my eyes from the ball at the center of the room, instead thrusting my arm towards the quartz on the table. Just before my fingers grasped the stone, I caught sight of a thin scar on my index finger and stopped.

Andrew and I were bonded. The same person in different times. When one of us injured our finger, the other did too. When I showed Andrew the dangers of the world outside, he stayed indoors, just like me. And now, when Andrew had constructed a life like mine, he died.

I caressed the scar with my thumb. Was what happened to him guaranteed to happen to me? What action had he taken that caused his death in the first place, and what's to stop me from stumbling into it too?

I had to take action. I carefully pulled the outer crystals away and ended the signal. I knew in my gut behaving normally would get me killed. The room was starting to spin, and I felt the urge to do something quickly. I thought for a moment, then grabbed the crystal ball. My fingers burned as I gripped its slick surface, but still I held on, raising the ball over my head.

I dismissed images of shattered crystal lacerating my legs and cutting up the curtain. No time for fear. With all my might, I swung my arm down and let go of the heavy ball. There was a blast of light, and the pieces spread everywhere. Once I blinked away the brightness, I looked down at my feet.

There was nothing left but debris. A few thin trails of blood trickled down my leg, dodging the scorched hairs. Normally I would have been deeply concerned, but now, it didn't seem so bad.

I tore down the curtains and threw away my supplies. The practice of divination is meant to give one a vision of their future. Now it seemed I got that vision every night when I closed my eyes and saw Andrew lying lifeless on his desk. I kept the blood-stained quartz for a few more days. When I finally built up the courage, I returned to the old hiking route, a road that ran with the cliffs. Standing at the edge of a great cliff, none of it frightened me quite like it used to. Whatever fear I used to have of a sudden death, I was far more afraid of going back to who I was and ending up like my dear friend. A tear ran down my face as I removed the wrapping around the quartz, gripped it tightly, and lobbed it into the abyss.

CHALLENGE ACCEPTED

Danielle Harward

Clint shook the acrid blood from his blade as it collapsed back into his robotic arm.

An alien beast known as a Rackzee lay at his feet. Its long catlike limbs and razor-sharp claws were currently stained with dried cow's blood—the farmer's livestock. Like most of this species, the Rackzee's fighting style was easy to predict: hide and then pounce. Once Clint found it crouched in the farmer's barn, his energy gun stunned the thing before it sensed his presence. Third code of all hunters: end it quickly and without suffering.

"I can't thank you enough," said the old farmer, wringing his hands as he looked between Clint's face and the Rackzee. He stood with one of his workers, who managed to inspect the dead creature while leaning his body away. "Damned thing took out more of my livestock than I care to admit."

"Sure. And my fee?" Clint said as he wiped his hands with a cloth.

"Oh! Of course. A hundred turpins, like we discussed."

Annoyingly, the turpins would need to be exchanged for galactic credits, so they could be used on any world, but he had a guy for that. And it was faster than waiting for this old farmer to figure out how to convert the currency.

The farmer looked pained to hand over the bag of square coins, but Clint paid no mind. He was used to that look. After all, he was one of the best hunters on this side of the galaxy, and his services were expensive.

Turning on his heels, he left the farmer to deal with the corpse. He had taken one of the Rackzee's teeth and added it to the leather cord around his neck to join various others dangling there. It was the tenth necklace in his collection and almost full.

"He isn't very pleasant, is he?" Clint overheard the farmer ask as he walked away.

Too often humans forgot about hunters' heightened senses.

"It's not his job to be pleasant," said the worker.

Paying no mind, Clint trudged away through the fields and farmlands on the way back to his ship. Corn swayed in the wind next to a field of crawling Pricklex, a small, sweet melon many used for dessert. In this galaxy, this small farming planet along with five others were situated closest to the sun. The other more industrial and residential planets were further away, braving harsher temperatures.

He stepped onto his ship's ramp, rolling his shoulders as he took off his gear. It was a personal vehicle, slim and spacious for one. Its silver sheen was ostentatious in Clint's opinion, but it could make interplanetary jumps fast enough for him to do a few jobs a day.

He appraised the necklaces hanging on the wall, each packed with teeth. Not all hunters took trophies, but for Clint, they were memories. Like pictures of a loved one.

His old leather chair creaked as he sat at his desk. He tapped away at the smooth console and recorded his log. Another Rackzee—at least the tenth in the last two months. He made a special note of the planet and its quadrant. In this shared database, hunters like him had spent years cataloging alien spawnings and their locations, creating a quick reference for what they may be dealing with when on each planet.

Rackzees usually stayed on the galaxy's outer rings, but they seemed to be moving inward, no doubt lured by livestock and lower security. Hunters like him would need to keep an eye on neighboring planets before the breeding got out of hand.

A hunter's job was to protect humans and their settlements—

and be paid well for their service. He would prefer to do that before more deaths. Scoping out nearby planets would likely help stop the spread.

A message icon blinked red in the right corner of his screen. He finished his log and then tapped the notification. The dark screen filled with lines of white text.

A new job.

After he plugged in the coordinates, his ship launched into the air, piloting itself. It would take him four hours to get to his destination. He typed back a quick reply to his new client, Doreen, to let her know when he would arrive.

He leaned back in the control center chair, buttons and switches blinking all around him as the stars rushed by. Eventually, he would take the time to clean up, change his shirt, and wash the blood off. But right now, he wanted to review the previous hunt—a benefit of having cameras in his irises. It was a way to check himself. To verify that he hadn't missed anything.

With the tap of a few buttons, the video feed of his hunt flickered to life. He ticked off the hunter guidelines as he watched.

First, ensure innocents were out of the way during a hunt. He'd held the perimeter with small drones. Second, explore the area, seeking to understand all aspects of the creature: its size, what it likely used as weapons, how it hunted, how large its teeth and claws were, etc. Seeking to understand before an attack both aided in his chances of survival and in ending the beast quickly, which was the third rule. If possible, don't let a creature suffer. According to his feed, this hunt of the Rackzee had gone perfectly.

Of course, they didn't all go that way. With a flick of his wrist, the video feed rewound to a week prior. The sanctity of this hunt had been ruined. The beast was called an Utoor by the locals, but little information about it was recorded in the hunter database. It had claimed an area of land, waiting for prey to come near. Sensitive hairs grew from each of its tentacles, alerting it of nearby prey. It had been almost impossible to sneak up on.

What Clint hadn't realized was that the beast's tentacles were acidic. The kill hadn't been quick, and it suffered as a result.

Having seen enough, he made his way to the back of the ship, ducking under wiring to get to the shower. He washed, taking his time to rid each speck of blood off his skin. He had learned the hard way that the sight of gore only further separated him from what people saw as "human." He personally didn't mind the separation; he was different from them after all and didn't want to pretend otherwise. However, it made interactions with humans difficult, to say the least.

He supposed he had been made to look good by human standards. Maybe it was meant to make him more like them. But instead, it only alienated him further because his body was the perfection most humans would never achieve.

The bio enhancements hadn't been painful. At least he couldn't remember any, but perhaps that was the design of his creators. In fact, he never remembered being anything but a hunter, though logic said he had lived a life before doing so.

Hunters seemed to simply wake, fully grown and ready to hunt. Only twelve existed at any time. Another would always be created when one died. And death only occurred when a hunter was eaten or torn to shreds, unable to be put back together.

As Clint scrubbed under his nails, he tried to remember the last time he had seen another hunter. Though they constantly shared information between each other, they rarely messaged or worked together. Five years and three months ago. Yes, another hunter and he had taken down a particularly unwieldy Barox together.

The ship descended. This planet would be colder than the last, not that the temperature would bother him.

As he dressed, his information database ran through the alien beasts who had been slain on this planet in the last few years. Last time he was here in the dead of winter. It was summer now, so there likely would be a lot more frustrating foliage to stomp through.

The ship completed its descent. He slung his rifle over his

arm, put his stun gun at his hip, and flicked his wrist, extending the knife hidden in his forearm.

The door opened to the new world beyond. . .

A woman waited for him outside. This must be Doreen. Dressed in wrinkled mining clothes, she clutched her hands so hard that her fingers might just fall right off. "Are you Clint? The Hunter?"

He gave her a nod. "Tell me what happened."

But his eyes never met hers. Instead, he assessed his surroundings. The heavy foliage would likely be difficult to move through. Large trees towered above them with leaves as long as his leg. The creature would likely be larger than usual. The air had an acrid tang. Fruit maybe? Based on the purple balls rotting on the ground. The wind shifted, and the unmistakable stench of blood filtered in from the west. Likely where the incident happened.

The woman swallowed hard, glancing at the knife jutting out from his wrist before looking back to him. "I've heard of the hunters' skill. Some say your senses are heightened. Is . . . is that true?"

At last, his gaze landed on her. "What happened?"

She blushed, dropping her eyes. "We mined the land out to the west."

Clint nodded; he had smelled correctly then.

"A creature attacked, and no one made it back. We didn't even realize until the miners didn't come home. That's when . . . when we found them."

"Were any alive?"

Her lips turned down in disappointment. It wasn't the first time a human was bothered by his lack of pity, but he wasn't here to mourn over the dead. He was here to hunt. And he needed a witness who could tell him what had happened.

"Um . . . no," she admitted. "Not by the time we got there. But some were missing from the camp. They might have made it out."

"Understood. How far west?"

"About three miles. Do you think you will bring back the others?"

He contemplated the notion. The likelihood they were already dead was high. "If I find any survivors, I will bring them back for fifty more turpins per head." The usual fee for survivors.

She nodded, her disappointment turning into contempt. Another expression that wasn't new to Clint.

"I'll let you know when it's done."

"Um . . ." She began to say more, but a piercing look from Clint had the words stumbling from her mouth. "I—I didn't tell you where you can find the village."

"No need. I'll find you," he replied. It was better than saying I can smell you. Her lilac shampoo would be easy to follow from a mile away, and if he did this fast enough, he could return to his ship and track her from here. But he doubted that would be necessary. With the way she spoke of the mine in the west, it was likely west of the village too. In fact, if he waited for a harder breeze, he wouldn't be surprised if he could smell the village.

She gave him a quick nod and turned to scurry away when he added, "I'll expect the full payment upon bagging this creature. A hundred turpins is my minimum fee, plus whatever survivors I find."

She paused, seeming to tally the money in her mind. "All right. We will have it ready." She disappeared into the forest.

First, keep the humans safe.

He flipped open an electronic messenger, which gave him access to the planet's video feeds and quickly typed a message to warn all humans to stay away from the western mine until further notice.

Satisfied, he moved in the direction of the mine, taking his time to get to know the foliage, the smells, and the colors of this planet. He let his senses adjust to the new environment, so he could better sense if something was wrong.

Hunters died because of their mistakes, so Clint did everything he could to avoid them. It was why he had lived a longer life than most.

His eyes roved the landscape. The flat, hard dark ground was filled with veins of the combustible ore which was mined here. The towering trees made his sightlines difficult, so he launched a small drone from his shoulder and sent it on a ten meter perimeter sweep.

The smell, though acrid, also held a sense of something akin to basil. The back of his mind scanned through the hunter database but came up with nothing. Perhaps something new then. The corner of his mouth turned up at the challenge. He would need to take care.

The stench of human blood grew closer, so thick that he was sure even a human could sense it. He came to the edge of a tree line and stopped, allowing the foliage to cover him as he peered into the area.

It was a massacre.

Blood seeped into the ground from fifteen bodies. His gaze darted from body to body, cataloging the wounds and the destruction around them. From the large injuries, he could tell the miners had died quickly. He didn't need to get closer to know they were fatal. Some bodies lay next to shovels or slumped over mine carts. They likely hadn't seen the attack coming or had time to prepare. Many carts weren't just overturned; they were crushed, as if one of the creature's paws was enough to break them apart. This was quick and efficient work.

The creature was large. And fast.

Clint's eyes followed the trails of blood, marking where the miners had tried to make a stand. There, he needed to get a closer look.

Checking his drone, he scrolled through its feed to confirm that it hadn't picked up any movement. To be safe, he drew his energy gun into his empty hand and stepped into the camp.

It seemed the miners had tried to stand back-to-back. The creature must have circled them. The men's glassy eyes were wide, their mouths still contorted into screams. The smell of the gore stung his nose as he picked his way through the shredded bodies, inspecting each one. They had deep gash marks. So the creature must've had claws. One man's leg was in half, and bite marks traveled around his knee, likely dragged before the creature ripped it off. The marks suggested the largest tooth was likely five inches long—a worthy addition to his collection. And from the tracks, he counted six legs.

Among the scent of death and blood, the basil smell remained. He saw no sign of the herbal plant on any of the miners here, so it was likely the scent of the creature.

Past the torn bodies, he found prints, as large as satellite arrays, leaving the camp. Before following, he measured the size and depth of the creature's footprints with his scanner. The weight of the creature was significant. And with how lithely it moved, he guessed its legs would probably come up to his shoulder.

The database didn't recognize the measurements he had taken. Neither in its bite size nor its paw size. A few creatures came close. The Vex, for example, a creature with a head that opened like a lily from hell. Or the Kikerat, a badger-like alien that liked to make its home in lava pools. But neither of those creatures fit all the aspects of the one he was dealing with.

It would be a new log then.

With practiced skill, his fingers danced over his energy gun, turning dials. The weapon crackled to life, powered to the max. He had a feeling that he would need the extra energy for this hunt.

To the left, birds launched into the sky, screeching in their wake. In half a heartbeat, Clint spun, pointing the gun upward. Peering through the scope and lowering toward the tree line, he listened. He scanned every tree, every crevice, and every leaf. Watching. Waiting.

But no creature appeared.

He breathed deeply, searching for any change in scent. But he was upwind, and even with his heightened senses, he couldn't reverse the weather.

He sat. Still and ready. Muscles tense and finger lightly on the trigger.

Seconds passed.

Then minutes.

Clint slowly lowered the gun. Keeping an eye out, he sent a second ping to the nearby town's video feeds for all to remain indoors. This creature was crafty, and he needed to ensure it was only him and the beast out in the woods.

His attention turned back to the scene at hand. The creature must have left the camp and headed north, following human footprints. Likely chasing those who'd decided it wasn't worth the fight.

His feet sank into the soft mud as he followed the tracks north. The footprints were fresh, and the foliage had been broken along the way. The damage looked to have been done by the humans in their desperate attempt to escape, not the creature. It hadn't followed in a straight line but weaved in and out of the path, maybe to avoid harming the plant life.

What a beast!

Clint's body fell into the familiar movements of the hunt. Feet planted on the ground and senses alert, he continually scanned the landscape and cataloged each new finding. He was alive. This was his purpose.

He came upon a body. The poor bastard had been sideswiped, which had sent him careening into a tree. If the blunt force hadn't crushed his skull, he likely would have died from the claw marks on his chest.

A pattern emerged. The creature didn't attack from behind as many did. In fact, most of the bodies left at the camp had bites and claw marks on their fronts. Interesting.

The next body he came across still clutched a small knife in his hand. Likely a desperate final attempt at protection.

The men's trail ended in a bloody pool thick enough to bathe in. Beyond that, no more human tracks remained. No more bodies to examine. Not even a scrap of clothes or a discarded limb. He circled the scene again. The creature's tracks led off to the east. Something had sparked a change of direction.

Clint narrowed his eyes. What was it up to? Even his drone couldn't pick up any more tracks. He called it back, and it clicked down into his shoulder.

He chuckled. His quarry was a smart creature. But not smart enough. He breathed deeply in each direction until he smelled it. Basil. Aromatic yet off-putting since the scent was now associated with blood. And stronger than it should be with the age of these tracks.

The creature was close, even if his enhanced vision hadn't tracked it yet.

He slowly turned, scanning the land around him. Every leaf and bush could be potential camouflage for the dangerous creature lurking in the forest. The bugs with their constant clicking had stilled, seeming to wait for something.

Clint stopped turning. It was only on intuition's whisper that he knew he must be looking in the direction of the creature. He felt it looking back at him. Yet he could not see it. Not a scale or a puff of fur out of place from the foliage.

A deafening scream ripped through the air. Human. A sound one only made in extreme pain. It came from further east, deeper into the forest.

He darted through the leaves, branches whipping at him just as the creature crashed through the underbrush to his right, heading the same direction.

Now that it moved, he caught a glimpse of its fur, the same brownish gray as the forest floor's dirt. He glanced between it and his path ahead, remembering the man who had been sideswiped. As the creature bounded closer, Clint clenched his jaw. That trick wasn't going to work on him.

When the creature was close enough for Clint to see its bright green eye, he let off a shot that went wide. It was enough, however, for the creature to drop a few feet back.

He smirked and kept running.

The scream echoed ahead once more.

Clint's lungs burned. His heart thudded. He ran with one hand in front of his face to deflect the branches and the other pointing his pistol in the air as he played the coming scene in his head.

Get to the human first. Pivot to face the creature so that the human was behind him. Make the first attack when it bounds out of the bush. Try to get an under-jaw shot with the energy gun to stun it if possible. If not, drop the gun and allow for close combat to sink the knife deep. Put the knife through the creature's eye.

Adrenaline pulsed through his veins as the creature bounded up on his left side and let out a gurgling hiss. Clint snarled back, careened right, and popped off another shot in its direction. Leaves and brush rippled as the creature veered away from him. Disappointment flared in him as it ran away. Chasing it off was the exact opposite of what he needed. He slowed as he came to a break in the tree line.

In the clearing ahead, half a man lay on the ground. He groaned, reaching up to Clint with shaking, bloody hands. How he was alive, Clint didn't understand. Intestines splayed out behind him as he struggled, gurgling blood. His spine stuck into the dirt like a tail. His eyes gave a silent plea. Not for help, Clint realized, but for a quick end.

Clint took another step, the wind shifted, and he smelled it. Basil.

The creature dropped from a tree above the dying man, landing on top of him. One of its massive paws—the size of Clint's hand—slammed into the man's head with a sickening squish. His silent request fulfilled.

Now it was just Clint and the creature.

Seeing it in full view, Clint's mind worked quickly to catalog its body. A head shaped like an owl's looked down upon him. Varying shades of brown and gray made up its fur, which looked closer to feathering. Its teeth and claws looked like broken, jagged pieces of wood, as if they would leave splinters with every rake. Its eyes, however, garnered Clint's focus the most. He recognized cunning in those eyes. A quiet calculation as it watched him. No creature had ever looked at him like this before.

As his mind tried to make sense of it, the creature waited. A great cliff towered above, leaving no room to escape, and Clint realized his first mistake.

The victims had been killed quickly with as little pain as possible. He now saw that it had been the creature who disturbed the birds back near the mine. How long had it been watching him? Learning and studying him before ultimately leading him here, with his back against the wall.

Pieces of the hunt came back to him as they watched each other. The bodies clawed and bitten but never eaten. The man under the creature's foot had not gotten here on his own. He had been placed here. And that chase . . . it wasn't running with him to try and beat him to its prey. It didn't care about the man under its paw. No. The way it had jumped closer and then veered away when he turned . . . It had herded him.

It wasn't hungry.

It lured him and trapped him.

It was a hunter.

Shuffling ruffled the bushes behind the creature, and out peered a miniature version of the thing. Offspring. The pieces fell into place.

Fear like he had never known before crept up Clint's spine.

The creature took one smug step forward. Then another. An unspoken challenge. A test of will between the two hunters to see who would give their first move away.

He would not be deterred. This beast may be protecting one of its own, but he had a job to protect the humans it slaughtered. One he was dedicated to. One he lived for.

The creature's eyes alighted with his same determination. Devious bastard. It tracked his every movement. What felt like whole years passed around them as they watched each other. But the sun and clouds hadn't moved.

Enough waiting. They lunged. Teeth bared. Gun aimed. Slamming together in a tangle of limbs and claws.

Clint got one shot off into the creature's stomach. In turn, it roared and lashed out with a claw, sending a spike through Clint's calf. He screamed and sliced out with his dagger, cutting through the woody flesh like an ax to a log.

The beast hissed and raked claws down his chest, sending him hurtling back. He tumbled and landed on a knee, gasping. His body burned like someone had set it ablaze, and blood oozed down his boots.

It whipped out with a spiked tale. Only years of honed reflexes gave Clint the ability to pivot to the side and slice down with his dagger. Now it was the creature's turn to scream. Where the pointed end of its tail once sat was a bloody stump.

Clint bared his teeth and stood. Dripping blood. Both his own and the creature's.

The pause was Clint's second mistake.

The creature unfurled before his eyes. First, the bark-like skin on its legs sprouted thorny spikes as long as his hand. Then it's back cracked, opening like a flower.

He was in deep shit.

He popped another bullet at the creature, which hit it square in the chest but didn't penetrate its thick thorns. It barely flinched. The wood on its back was now stacked like a shield, and four vines, pointed like the end of its tail, rolled out.

It stood to its full height, arching so Clint could see it in all its glory.

His fear came back. Along with something else: a sense of finality.

He gripped his dagger's handle as the creature launched itself at him. He let off another shot, grazing its face. It yowled but was not deterred as they crashed into each other. He sliced out wildly, aiming for its throat, but his dagger only nicked the creature as its thorns created a protective shell.

Wood-like teeth ripped into the soft flesh between his neck and shoulder, and two of its vined tendrils slammed into each thigh. Somewhere, his mind cataloged the depth of the bite, calculating the minutes until he would bleed out.

This was a killing blow. One he had seen dozens of times on

the victims of other creatures. His pulse slowed. Every heartbeat pumped blood out of his exposed carotid and onto the creature's tongue. Basil filled his senses until he choked on it.

He was dying.

And yet, he did not feel anger.

Fear, yes. But fear stayed alongside him on every hunt. So, fear sat beside him like an old friend as his body numbed, and his eyes grew heavy. Even as his conscious mind slowed, ambling to a full stop. He had no animosity for the creature whose jaws he now lay limp within.

It was, after all, a hunter.

KINDRED SPIRITS

Bryan Young

The Merriam-Webster dictionary defines the term "kindred spirit" simply as this: "a person with similar interests or concerns." Diving into the usage of the term and its etymology, it feels like it means so much more than that. The words separately originate from Old English and Latin, but the first recorded use of the term came in the form of a poem published in 1706. The book was called Horæ lyricæ: Poems, chiefly of the lyric kind. In two books. and was written by a man named Issac Watts.

> Were kindred Spirits born for Cares?
> Must every Grief be mine?
> Is there a Sympathy in Tears,
> And Joys refuse to Joyn?

It's no wonder that a poet brought such a phrase to the forefront of our lexicon because art raises the soul and awareness. But what was he asking for in this poem? What was he searching for? In the context of the larger poem, the poet, through Mother Nature, seeks the joys of others like them. And that is a common thing for humans through our experience from our cave-dwelling ancestors forward.

Kindred Spirits is the name of this collection, it's the theme of it, and all of the stories in your hand touch on this idea in some way, this need for connection. But this assembly of stories was also fashioned by a group of kindred spirits. The Infinite Monkeys are a chapter of the League of Utah Writers, and they have built a community to do things just like this anthology because they are united in a common cause. They're a group of people who believe in the transformative power of fiction. They found community rooted in the belief that writing can make the world a better place and that people are better when they are better connected. They have rallied around the idea that writing as a form of expression is important to our well-being as humans.

It's no small task to find a community of kindred spirits. You have to be ever vigilant, looking for just the right folks. And sometimes, you walk in and realize that everyone in that community is like a brand new old friend. That's how I felt when I first joined the League of Utah Writers. I'm the president of the organization, and I feel like I have well over 500 kindred spirits united to tell our stories and to find that sympathy of tears that Issac Watts wrote about more than 300 years ago.

We share our experiences with each other. We share our tears and our joys. That's what a community of any sort does. But writers find more kindred spirits. I would argue that a writer has more kindred spirits than most people because of what we do. We share our stories. We put those tears and joys and wonders and heartbreaks into a story and we pass that on to someone else, and they find themselves in the text.

How great is it to feel seen by an author?

How many times have you sat down and found yourself transported by a piece of art and got to the end and thought to yourself you knew the writer understood you implicitly?

That's one of the things I hope for, every time I sit down to read a new work.

The other thing I hope for is that the writer can make me a kindred spirit with an experience outside of my own. I want to see their grief and tears, and I want to sympathize. I want to be their kindred spirit to read their story and hold their hurt and understand it. I want to read about folks that are different than

I am, to see how life works for them—or doesn't—and I want to know their struggles. I want to feel their feelings. I want to share their concerns.

Yes, the textbook definition of "kindred spirits" is simple, but it embodies so much goodness in our world.

I hope that as you read this collection, you find new kindred spirits of your own. And, perhaps, you will be motivated to join a community of kindred spirits like the Infinite Monkeys—or really any chapter of the League of Utah Writers. And if you do decide to pick up that pen, I hope that I will be able to read your story and find that we are kindred spirits once I've read what your griefs and tears and joys and delights might be.

Kindred spirits were born for cares, and as long as we approach the stories we read in such a way, we will be that community of shared concern and make the world a better place along the way.

Bryan Young
President, League of Utah Writers
January 2023

ABOUT THE AUTHORS

Scott Bryan is the author of the Foresight Chronicles series available on Amazon from Big World Network. Currently, he's spending a lot of time as the scribe for a three-hundred-year-old vampire child, sharing tales of her endless battles with Dracula across history. He also searches the Multiverse, looking for fascinating narratives to share with this world. He's met lost fantasy creatures, demonic beings, time travelers, and Multiversal agents, each of whom has offered him stories to tell.

Scott is a member of the League of Utah Writers, Infinite Monkeys division.

You can find him on the web at http://night-children.blogspot.com/.

Gina G (she/her) grew up in southern Utah, where the summer sun spends the winter. Fate brought her to Washington state with its tall Evergreen trees, gray-blue waters, endless rain, and the city of Seattle. She fell in love with all of it.

Circumstances beyond her control brought her back to the coral-colored rocks of southern Utah and her family.

Every day she misses the rain.

Gina G is the published author of Secrets Cafe: The Appetizer, available on Amazon. She has published several short stories.

website: www.authorginag.us, Facebook: GinaG author, Twitter: GinaGauthor, and Instagram: Gina Gauthor

Danielle Harward is an author who enjoys spinning tales full of heroes and magic. Her work explores the difficulty of conquering inner conflict and the line between good and villainous themes. She owns and operates Alliance Ghostwriting, a primer ghostwriting agency aimed towards helping rebellious leaders author their future. She enjoys reading as much as she enjoys the archery range!

ABOUT THE AUTHORS

Katrina Hayes grew up in the forests just south of the Canadian border in Washington State. With no television or video games, books were everything. When she ran out of things to read, she stole the books her older siblings were reading and hid in the barn to read them as quickly as she could. She has a deep, voracious love for adventure in stories and tends to write following that inner love. She can't seem to help but slip a bit of magic, a little murder, or a little mystery into anything she writes.

Amanda Hill is an award-winning author with various publications in short story anthologies with the League of Utah Writers. When she isn't writing, she's volunteering in her local community, reading books of all genres, or knitting her way through closets full of yarn. She lives in South Jordan with her husband and five children.

C. H. Lindsay (Charlie) is an award-winning poet & writer, book lover, and housewife—not necessarily in that order. She spent thirty years volunteering as an event planner, helping organize and run SF&F and horror conventions, and a decade acting in community theatre. Now she prefers to stay home and write poems, short stories, and novels. She has poetry and short stories in 20 anthologies.

She's a member of SFWA, HWA, SFPA, and LUW. Mostly blind, she lives in Utah with her "seeing-eye husband" and a cat. She publishes her father's True Crime under Carlisle Legacy Books, LLC.

Inna Valerie Lyon is a Russian bumpkin raised on a steady diet of cabbage and potatoes peppered with the required reading of Chekhov and Dostoevsky.

During the day, Inna works as an accountant and specializes in producing colorful aging reports and cute collection letters.

At night, she writes stories about life, miracles, and cats.

Inna is a member of the League of Utah Writers, Blue Quill, and Infinite Monkeys chapters. She has a few writing awards for her essays and stories in different genres. She writes in both languages, English and Russian.

Inna lives in Utah with a big happy family.

Edward Matthews lives in Salt Lake City with his wife, two children, and two very noisy dogs. He toils out his days as a humble public servant. But when night falls, he retreats to his loft to scratch the itch of the dark things that inhabit his brain.

Whitney Oliver lives in West Jordan, Utah with her husband and three kids. She grew up in a small town in Southeastern Utah where she developed a love for the outdoors, a passion for words, and an obsession with telling her ancestors' stories.

Pat Partridge writes fiction (both short stories and novels), humor, and occasional nonfiction works. His book of political humor is in its third edition. He is the author of a mystery, Fragile Memories, and the road-trip novel Fast on Fifty. He is the winner of several awards from the League of Utah Writers. Recently, his short fiction—some humorous, some the opposite—has appeared in Remington Review, The Haven, Fabula Argentea, Ariel Chart, and anthologies. He has a restless mind and a fondness for all things funny. His goal for the year: write a perfect metaphor.

ABOUT THE AUTHORS

Steve Prentice is a writer, social worker, artist, and photographer. He is the Author of *Seventh Generation*, the story of a young man coming to terms with the death of his mother and his place in an ancient Cherokee Prophecy.

Steve studied art at the Art Student League of New York, Parsons School of Design and University of Utah. He has a Bachelor of Science in Sociology and a Master of Social Work.

Talysa Sainz is a freelance editor who believes life's deepest truths can be found in fiction. She runs her own editing business and spends her time at the library or volunteering with the League of Utah Writers. Always fascinated with the structure of words, she studied English Linguistics and Editing at BYU. She then went on to receive a Master of Science in Management and Leadership, focusing on nonprofit work, from WGU. Talysa is the President of the Utah Freelance Editors.

Lori Shields enjoys creative flow in visual art, music, and words. Currently, she is a member of two bands. She also enjoys painting, gardening, jamming, writing short stories, and dancing with her girlfriends. She has a BS in Women's Studies, an MSW from the University of Utah, and has walked across the country in protest of nuclear weapons. She is a member of First Unitarian Church, League of Women Voters, and the League of Utah Writers. She has been married for 25+ years and has two grown children. This is Lori's first opportunity to be published, and she is so thrilled she can barely stop giggling.

Logan Sidwell is a sci-fi writer and puzzle-maker from Utah. Although just starting on short story writing, he has already written and designed over 60 education simulations with Infini-D Learning, a "magic schoolbus"-like experience that challenges students to use their curriculum knowledge to

ABOUT THE AUTHORS • 185

solve complex problems. He strives to marry his background in Computer Science and his years of storytelling to create fun, compelling ideas that explore new ground in technological and fantastical settings.

Candace J. Thomas is a celebrated author of multiple genres, specifically fate-driven stories with fantastical elements. Her debut novel, Vivatera, won the Diamond Quill for Novel of the Year. Candace identifies as sapiosexual, which is obvious by her collection of Sherlock pop figures. "Brainy is the new sexy."

Johnny Worthen is an award-winning, multiple-genre, tie-dye-wearing author, voyager, and damn fine human being! Trained in literary criticism and cultural studies, he writes upmarket fiction, long and short, indie and traditional, mentors others where he can, and teaches writing at the University of Utah. www.johnnyworthen.com

Rashelle Yeates is a horticulturist who loves growing her own plants as well as seeing them grow in their native habitats. This has led to a love of traveling, experiencing as many different cultures as she can, and bringing that joy and experience into her writing.

Daniel Yocom writes about geeky things because people say to write what you know. Their love of the geeky, nerdy community dates to the 1960s through games, books, movies, and stranger things better shared in small groups. They're an award-winning writer and editor of short stories, books, and hundreds of articles published by blogs, magazines, and gaming companies.

They enjoy attending conferences, conventions, festivals, sharing on panels, and presentations. Currently serving as the president of the Infinite Monkeys Genre Writers, they want to help others become the writer/author they desire to be.

Join them at www.guildmastergaming.com.

Bryan Young is the President of the League of Utah Writers and an award-winning author, filmmaker, and journalist. He's done work in a number of licensed universes, including Star Wars, Doctor Who, Shadowrun, Robotech, and BattleTech. His latest novel is BattleTech: A Question of Survival.

You can visit him at www.swankmotron.com

J.E. Zarnofsky is a writer, larper, costumer, and all around fantasy enthusiast. She is always seeking new ways to tell heartfelt and collaborative stories. Apart from her day job in software, she can be observed in her natural habitats of coffee shops, ice rinks, or medieval(ish) battlefields—armored and ready with her sword or bow. Follow her online at jezarnofsky.com.